"Meant to Be"

A Lesbian Christmas Romance

Jenny Bloom

This book is intended for Adults (ages 18+) only. The contents may be offensive to some readers. It may contain graphic language, explicit sexual content, and adult situations. May contain scenes of unprotected sex. Please do not read this book if you are offended by content as mentioned above or if you are under the age of 18. Please educate yourself on safe sex practices before making potentially life-changing decisions about sex in real life.

This story is a work of fiction. Names, characters, businesses, places, events and incidents are the products of the author's imagination or used in a fictitious manner & are not to be construed as real. Any resemblance to actual persons, living or dead, or actual events is purely coincidental. Products or brand names mentioned are trademarks of their respective holders or companies. The cover uses licensed images & are shown for illustrative purposes only. Any person(s) that may be depicted on the cover are simply models.

Edition v1.00 (2019.11.25)
www.JennyBloomAuthor.com

Special thanks to the following volunteer readers who helped with proofreading: RB, Naomi W., Jennie and those who assisted but wished to be anonymous. Thank you so much for your support.

Chapter One

"Are you serious?"

Anna looked at the flight schedule to track her flight. As her eyes scan the board, she realized that the news wasn't good. Her one ticket out of there and back home had the big CANCELLED flashing right across the front of it. It was all due to the raging snowstorm happening outside.

Anna opened her phone, held it up and found her daughter's name in her contacts list. She opened it, and then typed out her message.

Anna: Hey sweetie. Mommy is trying to get home, but it might be a little bit. Be a good girl for Daddy, okay?

After sending the text, a feeling of regret coursed through her body. Anna hated being away from her daughter for any longer than necessary. She never wanted to leave Nina at home. While her ex wasn't a bad guy, Anna hated feeling like she was missing out on holiday time with her daughter.

"So, you're saying we're stranded here for another day?" a voice said.

"I'm sorry ma'am. There's a raging snowstorm out here. We only have power due to a backup generator. As much as I would love to help you get home, all flights are cancelled until it further notice," the airline agent said.

"Are you offering free tickets to those of us who are inconvenienced? the woman asked.

Anna noticed the fiery woman at the counter speaking to the agent. At first, Anna thought she recognized the woman's voice, but being away from home and in an airport, the odds of her running into a

4

blast of the past was not likely. Anna walked over to the woman, noticing her blonde hair, with bits of brown in parts.

"Is something the matter?" Anna asked.

The woman at the counter turned around and looked directly at Anna. Then Anna stared at the woman in disbelief.

"Lisa? Lisa Silvers? Is that really you? After all these years?" Anna asked in shock.

"Oh my God, Anna Jackson! I can't believe it. What an unexpected surprise! What are you doing here?" Lisa asked.

"I just wrapped up a business trip. Now, I'm trying to get back home. And you?" Anna asked.

"Trying to get home as well. It now appears we're stuck here for another day or so," Lisa spat.

"That's just great. I wanted to get home to my daughter," Anna said.

"Well, it isn't happening anytime soon," Lisa said.

"The airline is trying to secure hotel rooms for our stranded guests. Luckily we have several hotels at the airport. As soon as I have additional information, I'll update you. In the meantime, here are a couple of complimentary drink vouchers for you two. It might be a good way to take your mind off of things. Then as soon as I hear something, I'll make an announce," the airline agent said.

Anna knew the airline agent was just trying to do her job, but it certainly wasn't helping. However, she looked at Lisa standing next to her and flashed her a weak smile.

"It might be better than just sitting around here waiting. Then we can catch up on old times," Anna said.

Lisa smiled and agreed to have a drink with Anna.

"You're looking great. You're just as pretty as you were in high school," Lisa said

A small redness coursed over Anna's face. She didn't expect her to be so bold. Anna had been called pretty before, but she didn't expect it from her. Lisa was one of the most beautiful girls in school. She could have had the pick of boyfriends but didn't really go out with anyone in particular. She mostly ran around with other girls in school. Anna always felt a bit awkward around Lisa especially since she had a secret crush on her.

"Thank you. You look just like you did in high school," Anna said, almost breathlessly.

As Anna and Lisa stood near each other, Anna couldn't help but stare at Lisa. Suddenly, Anna found herself as smitten as she was in high school. It was one of those chance encounters that changes a person's life. Anna wasn't sure what to really make of her feelings.

"Anyway, I guess we should use these vouchers for something," Lisa said.

There was a small bar nearby. As Anna headed over, she noticed the proximity of Lisa's hands. It felt reassuring and nice. Anna wondered if this connection could mean something more. Then she had to be realistic knowing that her chance meeting with Lisa happened in an airport. Her school girl crush was years ago and daydreaming about a relationship now was just an unfulfilled fantasy.

When they got to the bar, they both sat down. The bartender looked at the drink vouchers in their hands.

"Ahh, I see they're bartering all of you with some coupons now. Hopefully the airline will also comp a hotel room for you too," he said.

"We'll see," Lisa said.

"What can I get you ladies?" the bartender asked.

"We'll both have red wine please," Lisa said. "Perfect. I'll get your wines. Would you also like some snacks?" he asked.

Lisa and Anna both nodded and smiled at the bartender. Then the bartender walked away with the drink order.

Anna sighed as she thought about her daughter and her desire to get home. She was deep in thought when Lisa broke the silence.

"I just want to get home. It's been one hell of a week," Lisa said.

"You're telling me. This is the last business trip of the year. Now, I'm stuck at the airport. I just wanted to get home and see my family," Anna said.

"You have a family?" she asked. She looked almost ashamed for what she said initially.

"Yeah. It's just my daughter and me right now. She's with her dad. We've been divorced for a long time. But we're still friends," Anna said.

"That's wonderful. I hope I didn't overstep my boundaries," Lisa said.

"You're sweet. He takes care of our daughter, Nina, when I'm traveling for business. I don't like it

7

when I can't help her though. I work a lot. She's a good kid, but I worry I'm not around enough. At least not in her early years," Anna said.

"I bet you're doing a better job than you realize. I bet she's a happy child who is excited to have you come back home," Lisa said.

"I just feel bad when I end up spending all my time at the office, rather than with my daughter," Anna said.

"Oh, I understand. I'm a freelance artist myself. While I'm not occupied with taking care of a child or a job, it's been quite hard for me to continue on for a long time. It's been a little empty," she said.

"So, you don't have any children?"

"Nope. I had a partner for a long time, but things happened. I'd rather not get into that. It's a sad story for another time," Lisa explained.

"I'm glad I came over to talk to you. The last thing I wanted was to sit here, all alone, for the next couple of days. This storm is terrible," Anna said.

Lisa looked out the window. The whiteout conditions was a beautiful sight, but also one that signified things wouldn't be easy for either of them for the next couple of days.

"It's beautiful, but it would be more beautiful at home in more comfortable clothes," Lisa said.

"That sounds heavenly. But, I have to say that it's very nice having you here," Anna said.

"If the airline does come through and find all of us rooms, I imagine we'll have to share. So, I would feel more at ease sharing a room with you. If that's okay with you," Lisa said.

Anna blushed. She didn't think Lisa was implying anything, but she still felt a little embarrassed by it.

"First, let's have a few more drinks," Anna said, her voice cracking.

"Fine with me. I figured it'd help us calm down, anyway," Lisa said.

"Yeah. We can also explore the terminal. There may be some shops opened at the moment. I also know that the airport has some sort of 'mini-garden' exhibit throughout the terminal. If you want to check them out, I would be happy to show you," Anna said.

"Sure. It's not like we don't have the time. Hopefully, we'll be able to get out of here within a reasonable time though. The snowstorm is supposed to last a couple of days. But we'll just get through it," Anna said.

Anna was still surprised to run into Lisa after all these years and in an airport at that. Hopefully, they'd make it home relatively soon. There was one last burning question Anna had for Lisa. After a brief second, she spoke.

"By the way Lisa, does this flight mean you're back in Monroe? Or, is it just a connection?" Anna said.

"Actually, I'm in Ashburn now. As you know, it's just a short drive from Monroe. I have a small apartment, but it's cozy. After leaving Monroe right out of high school, I attended State University. Then I just stayed on in the city. I've been back for just a short time. I was ready to come home after all these years," Lisa explained.

Anna couldn't believe what Lisa was telling her. Maybe it was something like divine providence giving her something she hadn't known she wanted.

"Well, I'll be dammed. You're living in Ashburn. I still live in Monroe. I inherited my grandmother's house when she passed away. It's a good place to live and raise my daughter," she said.

"Well, I'm glad that we're so close," Lisa replied.

"Indeed. It'll make the goodbye a little more meaningful later on, don't you think?" Anna said.

"Perhaps. But who knows. This may not even be goodbye. Maybe still a hello that's just the beginning," Lisa purred.

The way Lisa uttered those words to Anna made her blush. It was so perfect, almost too much for her to bear. In a strange way, she felt better than ever before. Maybe being stranded in the airport wouldn't be the worst thing to happen to them. There was something riveting about Lisa, and Anna wanted to learn more. As Anne moved in a little closer, Lisa didn't run away. Instead she inched closer to Anna as well. Perhaps this was what Anna had been waiting for, and what she desired more than anything else.

Chapter Two

The more Lisa looked at Anna, the more Anna reminded her so much of her lost love, Janice. It wasn't just the pretty hair, the gorgeous green eyes, and the way she spoke. Even Anna's mannerisms reminded Lisa of happier times in the past. A wave of sadness surged through her body as she thought about Janice.

"Although I wish it were under better circumstances, I'm enjoying catching up and getting reacquainted," Lisa said.

"It sure is. I need to stretch my legs. Would you like to take a walk?" Anna asked.

"I'd love that," Lisa said.

She got up, nodding to the bartender who took the free drinks coupons.

"By the way, the airport has given the okay to give everyone a complimentary meal. You are more than welcomed to eat here in the bar or you can go to the restaurant in the Gardens Hotel. It's the least we could do for keeping everyone trapped in here," the bartender said.

"Thank you," Lisa said.

"Yeah, thanks. Have you heard anything about resuming flights?"

"Just the same thing. They're hoping sometime tomorrow. It'll depend on the amount and how quickly maintenance can clear and de-ice the airport. We'll just have to wait and see," he said.

They turned, looking out the window at the entire place blanketed with snow.

"This is insane. I knew I should have taken an earlier flight," Anna said.

"It'll be okay. We'll get through it. Besides, if you had taken an earlier flight, I wouldn't have reconnected with you," Lisa replied. She liked telling herself that everything was going to be fine. It made the time a little easier on her.

"You're right," Anna said.

"It's a pleasure spending time with you. You know, you remind me of someone else I use to know," Lisa said.

What Lisa didn't say was that person from her past was someone who Lisa hadn't spoken about in a long time. Lisa looked at Anna, who smiled weakly.

"Anyway, we should probably walk around the terminal and check out the art exhibit. From what I've read, the exhibits are Christmas-themed. They even put festive lights around. It's a miracle how this place even has power, but I'm not complaining," Anna said.

"I'm not either. I'm just glad that we're here," Lisa said.

The other passengers didn't seem to pay much attention to them. Lisa felt liberated. It was the first time in a long time that someone who made her happy. Although Lisa hadn't seen Anna in a long time, she knew that Anna was a wonderful woman.

Anna had a cute frame, one that was small, but curvy. The way her eyes lit up when Lisa was around her. There was something about the current situation that made Lisa wonder if she's reading signs that aren't there. She knew it had been a while, but she certainly didn't want to do or say something stupid.

For the most part, Lisa was happy not being stranded in the airport alone. The last thing she would want to do would be sitting in an airport for hours doing nothing. Now, she had someone else to wait with.

When they walked around the terminal, they noticed that many of the passengers were out of sorts. They saw them sitting in lounges, on the floor or wherever a place could be found. Some people were on their phones making calls and texting. Others were trying to find electrical outlets to charge their phones. The talk among the passengers was all about their flights being grounded. Some of the store employees were trying to make the best of a bad situation.

"This is a whole different world," Anna said.

"You're telling me. It's so different when no one is ushering flights. It's amazing," Lisa replied.

"Let's just hope that flights resume as soon as possible. I guess for now we can check out the exhibits," Anna said.

Lisa knew there wasn't much else do other than visit the art installations. Lisa was enjoying spending time with Anna. When they both got to the center of the terminal, they noticed the skylight roof was covered in a white ceiling.

"Wow!" Anna said.

"It looks like the snow 'decorated' the place for us," Lisa said.

"Yeah. Under different circumstances, it would be absolutely beautiful," Anna pointed out.

Lisa almost said that it was almost as beautiful as Anna, but she stopped. She wasn't sure how Anna felt about those type of comments. It worried her slightly since Anna may not even be gay. Anna could be very straight and she just being friendly with Lisa. She just didn't know. Lisa looked at Anna and thought, *"That's the problem with some women. They 'seem' gay until they tell you otherwise."* Lisa had her fair share of women tell her that. While they appreciated her kindness, they weren't into women like that. It was sad, but that was the way things happened.

Anna was different though. The way she giggled and smiled, the way she sat close to Lisa without moving away or giving off a different vibe. It was all wonderful.

As they walked around the exhibits, Lisa had an idea. The flowers were beautiful. Lisa could see the grow lights that were scattered about, probably assisting with helping the little plants grow. But her hand twisted out, lightly touching Anna's own hand.

Lisa expected her hand to be pushed away. Instead, it was grasped, ever-so-slightly.

"I hope it's not too forward," Lisa said.

"I have to be honest, Lisa. I've never been with a woman before, but I know that I like women. I mean, I did have a child, but that was different. The two of us were too different. I know that the reason for us being together was originally for Nina. While my ex was a good man and a good friend, it just wasn't right," Anna said.

"That makes two of us who like women," Lisa said with a smile.

"Really? I would have never guessed. In high school, you were always flirting with the boys. I know you didn't date much, but I never really put two and two together," she said.

"That was a long time ago. But, I certainly knew that I liked women. I just had to keep it hidden," Lisa said.

"You're not the only one," Anna said.

"Once you get out into the real world and live, you realize what is and what isn't important. While I loved high school and the whole high school scene, I discovered the 'real' me in college. I learned to accept myself for who I am and not for an 'image.'"

"I never had the courage when I was younger. It was something I knew about myself but didn't pursue. I went to college, married and had a child. Now, I'm discovering the 'real' me as well," Anna said.

"Give it some time. Everything good come to those who have the patience to wait for it to come. Anyway, we have all night to chat. Let's walk and check out the art exhibits. They are magical," Lisa said.

"Yes, I certainly agree that it's a beautiful exhibit. Definitely worth it to share this view with someone as wonderful as you," Anna said.

The words made Lisa's heart skip a beat. While Lisa enjoyed the sentiments, she knew full well that she would have to leave Anna at the end when they got back to their normal lives. Lisa understood sometimes things weren't meant to last. However, Lisa was just happy to have someone near, even if it was temporarily.

"By the way, Lisa, once we finally get out of here and back home, is there any way I can contact you?" she said.

"Sure, we can exchange phone numbers. Since we live so close to each other, perhaps we can get together some time," Lisa said.

"Sure, I'd love that," Anna replied.

They exchanged contact info. Then they slowly strolled through the airport terminal in awe with the different pocket gardens and artist exhibitions. As they slowly walked around, they chatted about high school and where their lived ended up at that moment.

"For the first time in a long time, things are slowly beginning to make sense to me. I'm happier at this moment in time," Anna said.

"This is the first time in a long time that I've been happy myself," Lisa admitted.

"Really? You seem so 'put together' and confident," Anna said.

"Perhaps, but life hasn't been easy. Sometimes I wonder if I've missed out on things by holding myself back," Lisa said.

"My first impression of you is that you haven't held yourself back," Anna admitted.

"Thanks, Anna. But there are some things that you don't know about me yet, that I'm not ready to tell others about. But, let's just say that it's not easy for any of us," she admitted.

"It's not. I don't have it easy either. I love Nina with all my heart and soul. But, I've found out the hard way that raising a child is both wonderful and the hardest job I've ever had,," she said.

"From what you've told me, you sound like you're doing a great job," Lisa said with a smile.

"I appreciate your words. Sometimes, I don't feel like I am. Sometimes, I wonder if I'm even doing it correctly. I just do the best I can," Anna said.

Lisa paused to check out an exhibit of a Christmas tree made from dozens of red, white and pink poinsettias. The artist then draped the poinsettia 'tree' in white colored lights and silver garland. Lisa had to admit the artist had an eye for detail and was very creative.

Anna noticed Lisa looking at the exhibit and stopped to take a look at it. "It's so beautiful, don't you think? It's the spirit of the holidays on display," Lisa said.

"It is beautiful. With the holidays coming up so quickly, I don't have a clue where to begin," Anna said.

"I don't either. This is the first holiday that I don't know what I'll do. It's weird," Lisa said.

"I guess we're kind of kindred spirits in a way. Which is reassuring," Anna said.

Lisa nodded and looked into Anna's eyes. She felt an unexplained connection. It was different. It made Lisa wonder just what the future held for her. *Perhaps there are such things as Christmas miracles,* Lisa thought.

"Thanks, Anna. For keeping me company," she said.

"You're most welcome Lisa," Anna replied.

The tension between them was becoming unbearable. Anna was breathtaking. As Lisa started to close her eyes, she did the one thing she never thought she'd get to do.

Lisa kissed Anna.

Chapter Three

As Anna pulled back, she looked at Lisa with an incredulous glance.

"Did you just—"

"I did. Sorry about that," she said.

"No, I'm not mad at you at all. Actually, I must confess that I've had a secret crush on you since high school," Anna said.

"Really?" she asked.

"Yeah. Sorry I'm a bit awkward. I haven't been close to anyone in a long time," Anna admitted.

Anna blushed as she confessed both her secret crush and not being with anyone.

"It's been a while since I've felt like I do at this moment myself. I guess if we're confessing secrets, I remember fantasizing about you in school. I was just a bit confused doing those years," Lisa said.

"I think it's normal. I'm flattered that you thought about me as well. I never quite felt like I was part of the 'it' click. I was always a little unsure of my looks," Anna admitted.

"You were a beautiful girl in school and you're a beautiful woman now," Lisa said.

Anna smiled and sighed. It felt good to finally admit to herself and to Lisa and unburden the secret passion she has held inside for many years.

"Thanks. I've already said this once, but I am so glad we reconnected," Anna admitted.

"I am too. If you want to spend more time together, I would love that," Lisa said.

"That sounds good to me. Perhaps you'll be able to meet my daughter, Nine. A I'm sure she'll love you," Anna replied.

"I'm sure."

Lisa grabbed Anna's hand and held it as they walked around the terminal, looking that the exhibits.

"The lights they put around here look gorgeous. I'm impressed with how they decorated this place," Lisa said.

"I am too. It's a treat," Anna replied.

"Do you believe in love at first sight? I don't know if there really is such a thing. I really don't. If there is, then you're the first person I've had that sort of instant connection with," Lisa said.

"I don't know either. I've tried the dating apps and websites, but they just didn't do anything for me. So many on the personal ads are just one-night hookups. They are really interested in other than sex. I don't really understand dating. But I will say, this is quite a good date, if it is one," Anna replied.

"You're telling me. I was in a long-term relationship myself. And while I've been out of the dating scene for a while, it's still different to me," Lisa said.

"Well, maybe we'll both learn about the differences as we go along," Anna said.

The smile Lisa gave to her warmed her heart. Anna felt like a new person when she was around Lisa. She hoped Lisa felt that same energy. After a little while, both of them then sat down on the bench nearby, looking up.

"I do believe in fate. Maybe our meeting is some sort of fate," Lisa said.

"As do I. Thankfully we again live close to each other. Once we get home, we can make plans to get together," Anna said.

"That we will," Lisa replied.

"Spending time with you is so delightful. It's a refreshing thing to feel," Anna said.

"You're telling me. I don't really date. I tried meeting up with a few women. The women I've met were so catty and dramatic. A few of them weren't even 'out' to their families. Dating needed to be all hush-hush. Are you like that?" Lisa said.

Anna tensed, unsure of how to explain it.

"My daughter doesn't know, but my ex-husband does. He's definitely supportive of me finally moving on. He doesn't want to see me unhappy either," Anna explained.

"Ahh, I see. Well, I'm glad that there isn't any 'hiding' in public to be with you," Lisa said.

After a little bit, Anna looked at the time. She noticed it was around seven in the evening and she was hungry.

"We've talked so long I didn't notice what time it was. That isn't something that happens every day," she teased.

"I'm glad you like talking with me as much as I do you," Lisa said with a smile.

Anna grinned. For a moment, neither of them said anything at all. It was a nice moment together. Anna wondered just what may happen next. She dared to quietly think *What could a future hold for us?*

Anna would leave it up to fate. After they got up, the two headed to dinner. Then, Lisa smiled.

"I'd love it if you have dinner with me," she said.

"I'd love that a lot, Lisa. I really would," Anna said.

Lisa smiled. She was just happy to feel alive once again and not held back by the traumas of her past.

Chapter Four

Lisa was excited for the first time in a long time. She was definitely ready for whatever came her way. However, Lisa knew that it may not be as she hoped. Rekindling an old friendship is one thing. Moving it a more personal level is another. Lisa confessed her secret as did Anna, but that didn't guarantee them any sort of relationship beyond friendship. Plus, Anna had a daughter and a life before they met. Then again, Lisa had her own life too. Lisa knew that Anna meant a lot to her already. But, she was a bit concerned by the short matter of time reconnecting with Anna.

Lisa wasn't sure how to really proceed, but she decided to let things evolve as they may. Lisa also had some personal things to talk to Anna about. She just wasn't sure how to start that conversation. Lisa decided to just leave things as they were. Then when the time was right, she would explain everything to Anna.

As Lisa and Anna were walking to the bar, , an announcement was made by their airline advising them that they needed to return to the ticket counter.

They arrived at their gate and saw a line forming to speak with the airline agent. They made their way to the line to find out the news they heard over the intercom system. Both hoped that they were able to leave, but neither wanted to say anything out loud, in fear of jinxing themselves.

Anna and Lisa waited in line for their turns speaking with one of the counter agents. Not long after standing there, the buzz came down the line that the airline was assigning them complimentary rooms in the Garden Hotel.

After standing in line for about fifteen minutes, Lisa heard the agent.

"Next in line, please," the woman agent said.

Lisa walked to her counter. Anna wondered what the arrangements were going to be. After a few minutes, Lisa turned and waved Anna up the counter.

Anna was a bit confused for a moment, but made her way to the counter agent. Standing by Lisa, the ticket agency said, "As I explained to Ms. Silvers, the hotel has a limited number of remaining rooms left. We are asking for passengers to take rooms in pairs."

Anna shook her head in agreements. Lisa looked at Anna and just smiled.

"Ms. Silvers has advised me that you and she are best friends and have agreed to share a room. I do need to get you're okay for these arrangements. Do I have that?" she asked.

Anna's voice cracked a bit before she said, "Yes, yes of course. That will be fine."

"Thank you. I've given Ms. Silvers a key and will now give you one as well." The agent handed the key card to Anna and smiled. "If you can Ms. Jackson, please sign here for me. This is the complimentary form we need to give to the hotel. Then I'll send it over to the hotel to check you both in," she said.

Lisa and Anna together thanked the agent and began to gather their things. Before they could leave, the agent said, "By the way, we were providing a complimentary dinner to our guests. You both can proceed to the hotel's restaurant. By the time you walk over to the hotel's entrance, you can check in and proceed to dinner."

They again spoke in unison by thanking her. They turned around and headed to the end of the terminal where the Garden Hotel was located. At least they had a room to sleep in and dinner to look forward to.

***

After they were checked into the hotel, they arrived at the restaurant in the lobby of the hotel. Lisa looked around and noticed there weren't many people around.

"Wow. So, this is it?" she asked.

"Seems like it. Most of the people who were trying to get home by other means left as early as possible," ," Anna said.

"I guess we seat ourselves," Anna said.

"Let's sit in the back, if that's okay with you," Lisa said.

Anna nodded, sitting down in the back corner. A server, one of the three working, came over and looked at them.

"Well, you ladies are looking lovely," the server said.

"As lovely as two ladies in the airport during a snowstorm can be," Lisa said with a scoff.

"She means well. Anyway, I'll take a hot tea," Anna said.

"Same here. And, I guess we'll have whatever is available on the menu," Lisa replied.

After he left, Anna sighed.

"I have empathy for the people who need to work right now. This storm is really something," she said.

"It is. I just hope that it doesn't knock out the power," Lisa replied.

"I doubt it. But still, it could. I mean, I do at least have someone I can spend time with. Better than doing this alone."

"You've got that right," Lisa said with a smile.

Dinner went by quickly, even though it felt almost surreal in a sense. Lisa certainly wasn't complaining. At the same time, she also knew that going home would end the adventure. Then, she'd go back to the reality of being a lonely artist.

Life was fun sometimes, and Lisa hated it. She wanted, more than anything in life, to the life that she desired and she chose. Not too long afterward, the server came back with their food.

The server asked them if they needed anything else. Both said no and thanks him for their dinner. He then said he would be back later to check on them.

As they started to eat in silence, Lisa watched Anna's eyes. She wondered why Anna was being so quiet, especially after their wonderful time together before dinner.

Lisa cleared her throat and said, "You seem so quiet right now. Is everything okay? Is there anything bothering you?" she asked.

"I'm okay. I'm thinking about life and all. I wonder where life will take me and where things will go. I sometimes wonder if I'm a good parent to my little girl. At least in the sense that I can easily take life into my own hands," Anna said.

"You're a great mom. I'm sure of it," Lisa said.

"Thanks. I don't know. It's those things that sit in the back of my mind sometimes. It really makes me think," Anna said.

"I do the same thing. Sometimes I wonder if it's fate, or if I am just lucky," Lisa said.

"Yeah. I wonder that, too. I feel lucky to have found you though. You make a boring old life a lot happier," Anna said with a smile.

"That I can agree with," Lisa said.

Their dinner went by without a hitch. Then the lights flickered, and suddenly, Lisa tensed. She looked at Anna, and she looked about too.

"What's going on?" she inquired.

"I'm not sure, but I think we should make our way up to our room," Lisa said.

They rose up and said goodbye to the server. Then proceeded to their room.

The entire time they walked to the hotel, they were silent. As they entered the lobby, they were greeted with a notice that the elevators were temporarily suspended.

Both Lisa and Anna read the sign. Lisa then said, "Great day for a walk up to the sixth floor."

Anna wanted to laugh. *Just one more thing to cap off a day filled with surprises.* Anna sighed and looked for the stairs. Luckily the stairs were next to elevators.

"Well, let's do it. Just think that we can have a nice shower once we get up to the room. Plus, it could have been worse if he had all of our luggage instead of our carryon cases," Anna said.

Lisa and Anna slowly climbed the stairs to the sixth floor. It didn't take as long as either one expected, but by the end, they were fatigued. It was stress for being stranded rather than the stairs.

As they arrived on the sixth floor, Lisa peered to the right, looking for a sign that showed which way their room was located.

They walked the hallway and finally found the room.

"Here we go. Perfect!" Lisa said. They found their room. Lisa used to key to open up the door. She held the door for Anna.

"After you," Lisa said.

Anna walked into the room unsure of being alone with Lisa would hold.

Chapter Five

When the door opened, Anna sighed in relief. It was a comfortable looking room with two beds, a small kitchenette area with snacks and water, if they needed it..

"Awesome," Lisa said.

"Nice. We are so lucky to get a deluxe room," ,Lisa said.

As Lisa smiled at her, the lights flickered on and off three more times, before shutting off entirely. The room was temporarily blackened until the generator kicked in.

Lisa walked over to the window and pulled back the curtains. "Relax, we'll be okay. I, for one, welcome the peace and quiet in here. We could have sex in here and not a single soul would know," Lisa said with a laugh.

"Tempting, but I don't think I'm ready for that," she said laughing, "I don't mind talking and seeing how things go."

"I'm just teasing you. I think we can keep ourselves willfully entertained. I definitely approve of being in here than on those seats. They suck," Lisa said.

"You're telling me. Sleeping on those is hell on earth," Anna said.

They laughed and chatted throughout the evening. Eventually they spread out on the couch. Lisa reached over and held Anna's hand. At first, Anna was shocked by Lisa's bold move. Anna still remembered the unexpected kiss and could still taste the sweetness on her lips. "Your hands feel nice and warm. It's a nice feeling," Anna admitted.

"Good. I'm glad I can make you happy, Anna," Lisa said.

"Once we get home, I hope we can stay in touch," Anna said.

"Why wouldn't we? Do you really think I'd just up and forget about you?" Lisa asked.

"No. It's something I sometimes think about," she said.

"Well, you don't have to worry about that. I'll be around. I'm definitely willing to stick around for a cutie like you," Lisa purred.

Anna moaned slightly. Lisa couldn't help but let out her own gasp of pleasure as she heard those sounds. There was something so arousing and sweet about hearing Anna like that and having her nearby. It reminded her so much of Janice.

Janice was someone she didn't want to think about when she was with other women. Sometimes, the brain was an evil thing.

"Are you okay, Lisa?" Anna asked.

"I am. I was just thinking about something. Nothing to worry your pretty little head over," Lisa insisted.

"Yeah. Thanks," Anna said.

For a long time, Lisa didn't say anything further. She didn't want to. The moment was too perfect. Then when Anna turned to her, a grin could be made out slightly.

"Lisa, I know this isn't the most conventional place to fall in love, but you make me happier than I've been a long time. In fact, over the moon. For the first time in a long time, I feel that way," Anna said.

"That makes two of us," Lisa said with a smile.

For a moment, neither of them said a word. They didn't need to. They didn't want to spoil the moment. Then, Lisa turned, laid on top of Anna and gave her a kiss. Anna immediately looked at her with widened eyes. As Lisa pulled away, she shook her head.

"Why'd you stop?" Anna asked.

"I feared I might be moving too fast," Lisa said.

"I don't feel like you are, Lisa. Maybe I'm being a little too optimistic, but I feel like you're different from the rest of the women I've met," she admitted.

"Then I'll continue. Together, we'll experience each other in the way that we want to," Lisa replied.

Anna smiled, giggling as Lisa started kissing her and relishing in the feeling of the touch. Lisa felt lucky to have reconnected with Anna. *Perhaps it's divine fate*, Lisa thought.

Chapter Six

A spark course through Anna's body as she kissed Lisa. Lisa felt the tension in her body as she kissed Anna back. The kiss that they shared, the way they felt and the way they shared the moment, was perfect. Anna didn't want to let the moment go.

When they kissed, it felt like a rush of energy. As Anna let her lips move with Lisa's, she relaxed against Lisa's. Anna closed her eyes, savoring the moment. A small sensation touched Anna's lips. She immediately groaned, opening her mouth slightly. Anna felt Lisa's tongue against hers, touching it slightly, making her shiver with delight at the sensation. As Lisa kissed with gusto, Anna felt a hand move against her sweater, touching her. When she felt her stomach become exposed to the air, Anna let out a small gasp, but at the same time, she enjoyed the coolness enveloping her skin.

It turned Anna on, groaning in pleasure as she felt Lisa move her lips downward, touching the very tip of her neck and lightly pushing against the very edge of her body. As she did that, Anna let out another small groan of pleasure. Anna loved the way Lisa subtlety touched Anna without any second thoughts. Anna moaned when she felt Lisa gently bite her neck. "I want to make you feel good," Lisa said, lightly teasing the shell of Anna's ear with a small touch. Anna let out a small gasp. Lisa immediately pushed her hips up at the sensation of her teasing Anna. Lisa was so skilled Maybe that was the reason it felt so amazing, but Anna wasn't going to worry about it. For now, she just wanted to experience the full sensation of Lisa's touches. As Lisa moved her hands up, gripping Anna's breasts and lightly touching them through the fabric of her bra, Anna let out a small whimper .

It was so different from what Anna was used to. She was used to having vanilla, boring sex with her ex-husband. While he wasn't bad in the bedroom, it was different from what Lisa was doing to her. The touches alone were enough to drive Anna wild, making her wonder just how she even got that far. Anna loved it. The little touches, combined with the heightened senses, made her let out a growl of pleasure.

Anna then let out a sudden gasp as she felt a hand lightly touch her crotch, which was covered by a pair of thin leggings. She blushed at the sounds she made, realizing just how loud she was. When she looked at Lisa, Lisa simply grinned.

"You don't have to be that quiet. Let it out. Even if there is someone right outside the door, listening in on what we're doing, just experience whatever is going on. I know that, even with all of it happening, it certainly can be a bit shocking. I promise you though, I'll make you feel wonderful," Lisa purred.

Anna nodded her head, agreeing to Lisa's words. Another hand moved upward. Soon, Anna felt Lisa move her lips down her body, touching the very edge of her neck, making Anna let out a small groan of pleasure as a result of it all. Lisa was too good, almost too much for her. As Anna felt the pleasure grow with every passing moment, she wondered what Lisa had in mind next, and what she would do now. Lisa then moved her hands upward, kissing down Anna's neck until she moved her lips down toward the outside of her breasts. Anna let out a small sound, suddenly surprised by the sensation of it. , She then let out a small cry of pleasure as Lisa moved her hands past Anna's bra.

"Your breasts are so lovely . Beautiful breasts on a gorgeous woman," Lisa said.

"God, you're so sappy," Anna said, blushing as she heard those words. Then, Lisa's lips touched the very edge of Anna's breasts, lightly sucking and teasing her. When Anna felt that, the heat and pleasure from her body suddenly shot forward, and she let out a small cry of desire.

The impact turned her on like no other, making her suddenly realize what was going on. Anna couldn't help but love and enjoy the sudden pleasures of the flesh. As she felt Lisa's hands and mouth against her nipples, she let out a small cry, feeling them get erect even though she couldn't see it. The feeling was perfect. Anna couldn't help but love it. She knew that Lisa was teasing her on purpose and turning Anna on and making her feel good.

Lisa's touches were enough to make Anna shiver. It felt so perfectly delicious. She didn't want any of this to end.. The words and sounds uttered from Anna's mouth were music to Lisa's ears.

She knew Lisa enjoyed it as much as she did. Every touch was enough to turn both of them now. Lisa was making Anna a breathing mess as Lisa continued her actions.

Lisa then took Anna's nipple into her mouth and began to suckle. Anna gasped once more of the sensation. It was something she had never experienced before.

"Do you like that? Do you like me sucking on your pink bud?" Lisa softly said to Anna.

"Oh God Yes! Don't stop! It feels amazing!" Anna remarked as her eyes rolled upward in desire.

She continued to moan as Lisa moved her hand down to Anna's moist and wet honey pot.

Lisa then softly bit and nibbled on Anna's nipple slightly, causing Anna to let out a cry of pleasure.

Anna looked down at Lisa and made eye contact. "Don't stop," Anna said, "You're driving me over the edge with desire!"

"As you wish," Lisa said, with a devilish grin. It made her want nothing more than to continue and to experience all of it.

Then Lisa began to rub Anna's heat in slow circular motions, rubbing her clit between her fingers. . "Oh God! Yes!" Anna moaned in desire. let out a small cry, flushing and holding her hands to her mouth, but then Lisa smiled.

"Did you forget that nobody is around to hear us?" Lisa inquired.

"It's just embarrassing," Anna said.

"I know. It's the best part of it though. The little embarrassing sounds that you make are adorable," Lisa said with a smile.

Anna blushed, but not before Lisa then moved her hands underneath Anna's pants. She let her hand dance against the very edge of Anna's honey pot, making her cry out with rapturous delight as Lisa continued these actions. Anna held onto the sides of the couch, crying out loud and in pleasure.

"Don't stop! Don't stop!" Anna cried out in ecstasy.

Every touch made Anna wet with desire. She knew Lisa was skilled, but she didn't expect her to be as good as she was. Between the tip of her thumb touching the tip of her clit, and Lisa's fingers pumping within, Anna was shocked at how amazing this felt. It was definitely better than what she ever imagined. Anna then felt Lisa push down, touching her g-spot. When Lisa did, Anna once again grabbed the couch and immediately cried out loud.

"I'm cumming! Oh God, I'm cumming!"

"Cum for me baby! Don't hold back! Cum for me!" Lisa said as she continued pleasuring Anna.

Then Anna felt the of rush of her orgasm as she panted and moaned with delight.

"Oh Lord," Anna said to Lisa.

"Good eh? I'm glad I still have my magic touch," Lisa purred, touching the finger to her lips and licking it seductively.

"Yes you do," Anna said, her voice breathless as she spoke to Lisa. There was something about it that made her want nothing more than to just feel the pleasure overtake her, making her cry out with delight, and with a need for more.

"Always, I guess that's that," Lisa said, moving off of Anna. Then Anna gripped her arm, looking up at her.

"Let me return the favor?" she asked.

"If you'd like but let me get my pants off. It's a little harder with jeans," she said.

Lisa slipped her jeans off. Anna noticed she had a nicely shaped backside, and a plump honey pot underneath her pants. Anna then moved her hand forward, touching and then slipping her hand in, lightly moving her hands and cupping Lisa's moist and warm heat.

"Oh God," Lisa said, reacting to Anna's hands. Anna then let out a small groan as she heard those sounds. She continued to tease Lisa from the inside of her panties, moving her fingers around the outer edge of Lisa's vagina. Judging from the sounds that Lisa uttered, she was definitely enjoying Anna's actions.

Lisa closed her eyes slightly as Anna worked her over. "It feels so fucking good! " Lisa moaned

Anna started to move her fingers a little bit faster, enjoying the sounds of delight that escaped Lisa's lips. Every single touch, every single movement, it was all coming together. Anna loved every moment of it.

She could tell that Lisa was enjoying it as much as she was. Lisa was enjoying all the touches and feelings. Anna began to move a bit faster, plunging her fingers in and out. When she pushed her fingers up to Lisa's g-spot, Anna could see that Lisa liked it by the sounds of pleasure escaping Lisa's lips. Lisa she soon cried out.

"Oh God! Don't stop! I'm cumming!" Lisa cried out.

Anna continued to finger fuck Lisa. Lisa then began to buck on Anna's fingers, driving them deeper into her needy hole.

"Yes, yes, yes!" Lisa moaned as she continued to ride Anna's fingers.

Before long, Lisa felt her organism overtake her. Lisa let out a loud groan and begged Anna not to stop what she was doing. Then Lisa's body began to rock and jerk as she came.

"That's it! Don't hold it back," Anna said.

Lisa was moaning and short of breath as she embraced the overwhelming feelings of her organism. Then she opened her eyes and noticed Anna staring at her with a smile of her face.

No words were spoken between them. There were no need for words. They were both wrapped up in the afterglow of the evening.

When she moved back, Anna felt Lisa curl up next to her. They both were felt happy and satisfied.

They fell asleep together. While an airport hotel wasn't the most ideal locale for making love and sleeping, Anna couldn't complain. She liked Lisa and she liked the way Lisa made her feel. Anna hoped things would work out and she would see more of Lisa. At least, it was what she hoped at the end of it all. Sometimes fate wasn't so nice to her. Things could be more difficult for them from here on out.

Chapter Seven

Lisa didn't mean to sleep with Anna as quickly as she did. She just wanted to cuddle with her, have a bit of fun kissing, and leave it at that. Waking up, Lisa's brain was a bit fuzzy. She rolled over and saw Anna staring at her and smile.

"Good morning. Hope you had a great sleep. You know, I could get used to this," Anna said with a teasing smile.

"I could say the same thing," Lisa purred.

The reality of the situation though, was that Lisa wasn't sure if she really could. After all, that would mean having to face the pain in her past so that she could move on. Lisa wasn't sure if she could do that yet. But, at that moment, having fun with Anna was what mattered. It made her feel younger than ever before.

As they lay in bed, the lights began to flicker on and off. Then finally, they came on again.

"Looks like the power is back," Anna said.

"Yes it does. We should probably get dressed and check on our flight home," Lisa said.

As they began to dress, neither one of them spoke. Lisa looked at Anna and noticed a worried look on her face.

"Is everything all right, Anna?" she asked.

"I'm fine. I'm just confused about what's going to happen next," she said.

"You mean with us?" Lisa asked.

"Yeah. I mean, I hope this wasn't just some one-night stand. That would be so wrong in so many ways,," Anna said.

"Don't worry. It wasn't a 'bam-bam thank you ma'am' situation," Lisa said.

Lisa was a bit scared of letting go of her past. She had never done something like this before. She wondered what Anna thought about it.

It was the first time she had made love in a very long time. Not since Janice was alive. A shudder coursed through her body as she remembered the woman from her past.

"Is everything okay with you?" Anna asked.

"Yeah. Just thinking," Lisa replied.

"About what?"

"About us. Anna, I haven't felt like this in a very long time. I'm just a little nervous. And, I don't want to disappoint you," she said.

"You're not going to. You have to do a lot to disappoint me," Anna said cheerfully.

That was where she was wrong, but Lisa would let her stick with that fairy tale for now.

"Let me call the front desk and see if I can get any update," Lisa said. She picked up the phone, but service was out.

"No telephone service. Well, let's walk to the gate and find out the status of our flight," Anna said.

***

They left the hotel and made their way back to their departure gate. As they walked the terminal, they noticed some of the planes had their lights on.

40

"I guess the worst of the storm has passed," Lisa said.

"Yeah. I guess so. Let's check with the counter agent," Anna said.

They went to the gate. As they made their way to the line, airline agent looked up and smiled.

"Oh, thank goodness you're finally here. The phone lines are down at the moment. We went to your room, but you didn't answer. Obviously you were making your way back here," the ticket agent said. "Listen, take your bags and check them in with the agent at the door. They're getting ready to depart," the gate attendant said.

"Sorry we held up the plane," Anna said, blushing madly because of the reason why she was late.

"We'll get on right away," Lisa muttered.

"I had you both on my roster. We weren't going to leave without you both. It's an open seating flight. You can sit where you want. It's not a full flight either. So, I imagine you two can sit together. You two seem like wonderful friends," she said.

Lisa almost burst out laughing at those words. *Friends, sure. Whatever you say.*

"Right. Anyway, let's board, *friend*," Lisa said, silently laughing to herself.

"Okay," Anna said.

As they walked into the plane, Anna looked at Lisa with a grin on her face. Lisa, however, was thinking all about what would happen now, now that she had fallen badly for someone.

"Wow," Lisa breathed to herself.

They got on the flight. Like the ticket agent said, it wasn't a full flight. It didn't seem like there were a bunch of children either. Only a couple teens napping in the back.

"This seems like a good flight," she said.

"Yeah, I'm just ready to get home," Anna said.

"Well, we'll be there soon. This was a fun little adventure. I'm glad that fate, or whatever you'd like to call it, brought us together," Lisa said.

Lisa knew it may not keep them together. So, she decided to cherish the moments as they came. Thinking about arriving home and parting ways, Lisa found herself deep in thought. Then she heard Anna's voice.

"Are you sure there's nothing wrong? You have my ear if you need to talk," Anna asked.

"It's nothing. Don't worry about it," Lisa said.

"Are you positive?" Anna said.

"I am. It's just been a long couple of days," she said.

"You're telling me," Anna replied with a laugh.

They sat next to each other on the flight. However, Lisa's mind was racing. She didn't know how to even start telling Anna everything. Maybe it was best for the best to take a wait and see position at the moment. Then she could figure out how to open up to Anna and reopen old wounds.

As the flight took off, Lisa felt a hand against hers. She stiffened for a moment, looking down and realizing it was Anna. Lisa almost called her Janice which would have been awkward for both of them. Thankfully, she was able to stop herself.

***

The flight was shorter than Lisa wanted. She wished she could spend more time with Anna. The trip was good for her mental health, but Lisa wondered if she was on the right path with everything. When the plane landed, she felt that irrational fear of what may happen next, of whether or not she would ever see Anna again.

When they got up, Lisa looked at Anna once more. There was a pause, and Lisa tried to figure out what to say, but then Anna shook her head.

"We can say our goodbyes when we get our bags," she said.

"All right," Lisa said, feeling a bit relieved. It wouldn't be the end for them.

When they finally got the baggage claim and picked up their bags, Lisa felt a bit apprehensive to say goodbye. She just hoped that the promise of keeping in each wasn't just words said in the moment.

"I have my ride picking me up outside. What about you?" Anna asked.

"I drove my car here. Since no one is here to pick me up, I should go ahead and go," Lisa said.

Lisa didn't want it to the end. She also didn't want to lose Anna. Before she could say anything, Anna simply grinned at her. She leaned in, capturing Lisa's lips in one last kiss. Then, Anna pulled back.

"I wanted to give you one last kiss. I hope you don't forget about me," she said.

"I don't think I ever will," Lisa said.

Anna nodded, blushing once more before leaving. Sometimes a person needed to take a leap of faith. Letting Anna walk away was Lisa's. Fate brought them together once. Will fate keep them together now?

Chapter Eight

Anna felt a sadness, a longing within her as she exited the terminal. She headed to her waiting ride. When she got in, the driver looked at her and could see a sad look on their face.

"Are you okay?" Anna's driver asked.

"Yes, I'm fine. I just have a lot on my mind. Thanks for asking," Anna said.

As the driver took Anna home, she wondered if Lisa would really forget her. She didn't feel that Lisa was that type of woman. But she was surprised that she didn't receive at least a goodbye text. She knew she might be reading too much into the situation. For whatever reason, not receiving at least a simple "goodbye" irritated her slightly. Maybe goodbyes were difficult for Lisa too.

When they arrived at Anna's house, she gathered her things, paid the driver and made her way into her house. She opened the door and set down her stuff. Then closed the door. She leaned against the front door and let out a big sigh. She looked at her cellphone just in case Lisa texted. Then she noticed that Peter had called and texted her.

"Crap," Anna said, looking at the calls and texts. She quickly hit redial for Peter.

"Hey. I just got home. It's been a hell of a week," she said.

"Sorry to hear that. Everything is fine here. Nina was just asking about you," Peter said.

"Let me catch my breath and I'll head over there right," she said.

Anna grabbed her purse and keys. She then headed out the door to her car. While she wished for a few minutes, she missed her little girl and just wanted to give her a big hug.

Not long after leaving her house, Anna arrived at Peter's place. Nina bolted out the front door, little red curls bouncing in the air and a beaming grin plastered on her face.

"Mom!" she said.

"Hey sweetie!" Anna said, hugging her daughter.

"Were you good for Daddy?" Anna said.

"Yeah. It was fun, but I missed you. He's a good daddy," Nina said.

Anna looked over at Peter, who was awkwardly shuffling against the doorway.

"Hi Peter," she said.

"Hi Anna. Glad to know you're back."

"Sorry, about the delay with the snowstorm and all," she said.

"You're fine. It was nice having Nina around for an extra couple of days Did you have a good time? How bad was the storm?"

"The storm was terrible. Thank goodness the airline put me up in a hotel room. I didn't relish the thought of sleeping in the terminal lounge. At least I had an old friend from high school to keep me company," Anna said.

"An old friend? That's amazing to travel almost across the country and meet up with someone from school. Who was it?" Peter asked.

"Someone you wouldn't know. Anna Silvers."

46

"Good thing for small miracles having a familiar face around to pass the time. I guess you'll take Nina this weekend?" he asked.

"Yes. That will give you a little break," Anna said.

"I'd like that. Thanks Anna," he said.

Peter hugged Nina and kissed her on the top of her head. Nina looked up at him.

"I love you Daddy! Thanks for always being there for me."

"It's my pleasure, Pumpkin. You be good for Mommy and I'll see you next weekend."

Anna and Nina walked to her car and got in. Peter waved good and then closed the door. Anna sighed. She wondered if she could talk to Peter. Then, Nina tugged at her coat.

"Are you okay, Mom?"

"I am honey. I'm doing all right," Anna said.

"Okay. I guess you're tired," Nina said.

"I am, just a little," Anna replied, smiling.

Anna had a lot on her mind to figure out. She wasn't ready to tell Nina the truth about her sexuality. And Nina certainly wasn't ready to be told about Lisa. Anne still expected at least a call or text. There was nothing.

When she got home, Nina went to her room to unpack and play. Anna put some clothes into the laundry. Anna wondered what would happen next. Anne had expected Lisa to at least communicate with her. When she put the last of her clothes away, she thought about calling Lisa and telling her that she was safe, but she didn't. Her hands dangled over Lisa's name. Then she shook her head.

"No, it's for the best," she said with a sigh.

***

After the laundry was done and the clothes were folded and placed on hangers, Anna walked to Nina's room with her clothes. Anna opened the door and walked in. Nina was sitting on the floor playing with her dolls and laughing. Nina looked up and saw the distant look on Anna's face.

"What's wrong, Mommy?" Nina asked.

"Oh, nothing. Just thinking about my trip," Anna replied.

"Did you have a good time?" Nina asked.

"I did. It was a long trip though. I was ready to come home a few days ago. But I got to spend it with someone who I use to know years ago. I thought she would text Mommy, but I guess not," Anna said.

"Hopefully they do. Once they do, you'll be happy again," she said.

Anna laughed and said, "Yes, that would be nice."

Nina went back to playing. Anna walked out of her room, closed the door and headed to her office. Anna checked work at her computer. That was when she saw an email.

Hey Anna. I hope you made it home safe. Boss wants you to do a show at the art exhibition next week. They're looking for investors, and your promotion's already making waves. Let me know if that works. It'll be next Friday at Seven.

Bill

Anna's eyes widened. *They already want me on another project?* That was insane. Then again, the investments the company she worked for were diverse, because that was what made the sales. She agreed to it, saying she would love to and pressed the send button.

Anna picked up the phone and immediately called Peter. She wanted to let him know of the situation. She wanted to make sure that he was fine watching Nina for a few more days. Peter enthusiastically agreed to it.

"You're such a good dad. Thank you so much," Anna said.

"I know I am," Peter said, laughing.

Then he said, "Anna, I know it's none of my business, but you need to find someone. I know you're lonely and work is a way for you to escape from the loneliness. I know we weren't meant to be together. But, Anna, I care for you and I want you to be happy."

Anna paused. "There is someone, but I doubt she will ever call me back," Anna said.

Anna didn't know if she would ever see Lisa again. She chalked it up to a "fling" and nothing more. Besides she needed to focus on the upcoming holidays with her family That was the way it was done.

Chapter Nine

When Lisa arrived home from the airport, she saw the pile of mail—either bills or requests for art. She put down her luggage, sat down and sighed. It had been a long time. She took a few minutes to relax and breathe.

Then she got up and walked over to her computer. She turned it on and went to her email account. Then, she saw email about the art show she was in next Friday, and the work she would showcase.

"Damn, that's next Friday. I thought I could catch a break," Lisa said with an annoyed tone of voice.

The loneliness of the house was eating away at Lisa. She continuously wondered whether it was right to pursue Anna. She has a child and an ex-husband. Lisa just didn't know how she would fit into Anna's life.

Then again, she always wanted a child. Raising one alone as a single artist wasn't her idea of fun. She worked on her art instead, living vicariously through that.

Still, she wondered how Anna was doing. Lisa opened her phone and found Anna's number. She thought about calling Anna, to find out what was going on, but she didn't.

"Nah. She's probably busy anyway," Lisa said.

That was the excuse she always used with women she saw. They were all busy. They would never have time for little old her. It was better this way. Or at least, that was what Lisa would tell herself.

She continued finding herself thinking about Anna and their time together. Maybe it was fate messing with her. Perhaps it was time to find love again. The whole situation was much too much at the moment. She needed a break. Lisa knew the exact place to go.

When Lisa got to the local bar, she saw Lauren working there. Lauren looked up and smiled at her.

"There you are. I've been missing my favorite regular," she said.

"I was stranded in an airport. Winter is rough," she said.

Yeah, you're telling me. What can I get you?" Lauren asked.

"The usual please," Lisa said.

"Coming right up," Lauren said.

Lisa smiled as the young bartender took care of her order. She wondered what Lauren was up to these days anyway.

"So, how are things?" Lisa asked.

"Good. Robert and I are doing well. What about you? Did you finally meet someone?" Lauren asked.

Lisa tensed, and Lauren looked over at her, immediately clicking her tongue.

"I knew it," Lauren said.

"What are you talking about?" Lisa asked.

"That look just now. You did, but you're worried about pursuing a relationship. So, spill the beans. Who is she?"

"Her name is Anna. She's someone I knew in high school. She lives in Monroe and has a young daughter. We reconnected in a very strange situation," she said.

"How strange are we talking?" Lauren asked.

"In an airport. We were both stranded and on the same return flight. We had dinner and shared a hotel room. Then, we went from there," she said.

"Oh damn. Well, is she cute?"

"Amazing. Really curvy body. Beautiful red hair, and that smile," she said.

"So, what's the problem?"

"I'm just apprehensive ," she said.

"Come on Lisa. You're older than I am. I know that you're holding back because of the past. When are you going to learn that the past isn't something to be scared of? Holding onto it will only make you miserable," Lauren replied.

"I know. Like I said, I'm worried," she said.

"I know you are. But how long has it been since Janice?"

"Almost two years, but you know how it is. These things take time. Time does heal wounds sure, but can I really recover?"

"Not with that attitude. Trust me, Lisa, you're only going to feel worse if you continue to hold back and feel miserable. It's been long enough. You will always love Janice and hold on to the good memories. You don't deserve to string yourself along," Lauren said.

"You're right. Do you think she'll understand what I'm going through at the moment?""

"Maybe. Who knows. She has a child though. Is that a problem with you?"

"No. I've always wanted a child myself. I don't have any parenting skills. Her daughter may not like me," Lisa said.

"Children are honest when it comes to make a parent's 'new' friend. If you're nice and friendly, then there shouldn't be a problem. Robert doesn't have any children, but I have dated a few people who have. Mostly a few women in the past who 'gave' up on men after having a child. Then they wanted me to be their 'lesbian' therapist," Lauren said.

"I've dated those types too. But Anna seems different. Anna has a good head on her shoulders, a daughter she adores and she's trying her hardest."

"Well throw caution into the wind and go for it. Why are you waiting? It's obvious your mind is made up," Lauren said.

"When the dust settles and she realizes I'm just a lonely depressed woman, what will she really think of me?" she said.

"Lisa, you can't continue to hold onto the pain of the past or the people you couldn't save. I know the past isn't, and hasn't been, easy but give yourself a break. Stop beating yourself up. I honestly think it's time to move on and move forward. You don't have to lose the past. Embrace it. I'm pretty sure Anna has a past, too," she said.

"Yeah, I guess so. I mean, maybe I just have to do some soul searching on my end," Lisa said.

"I think that's for the best. Anyway, enough about that,," Lauren said.

"Thanks, Lauren. If we hadn't been so different and wanted different things, maybe we would have found ourselves together. But, at least you're still a good friend," Lisa said.

"I'll always be here for you. I cherish you and our time together. I love you and always will. We just weren't compatible in that way," Lauren said.

Lisa nodded. She remembered after what happened to Janice, she leaned on Lauren for support. Janice had just died and she was so despondent. Lisa confused Lauren's comfort for something more intimate. However, Lauren gently let Lisa down and gave Lisa support and friendship instead. Lisa realized that not having that special someone in her life was slowly killing her. It was made her realize what was going on in her life.

"Do you think I can fall in love again?"

"That depends. I know it's close to Christmas, but don't rush it. Anna could be the one, though," Lauren implied.

Lisa nodded. "I want to believe she is, but I also don't want to push it. Why is it so hard? I shouldn't be so hyper-focused on everything. Maybe it's just my way of coping since I have a damn show in the next few days," she said.

"You should focus on the show. Then, figure out for yourself what you can do and how to go about making Anna happy. Otherwise, obsessing over everything will only make you feel worse," Lauren said.

"Yeah, you're right. I'll figure it out. I'm glad I have you, Lauren. You make things easy."

"Relationships are never easy, Lisa. Remember that. You and Janice had a very stable and loving relationship. The future is unknown. It'll be better if you're with someone who makes you happy," Lauren said.

"I'll remember that. I don't expect life to be a walk in the park, but you know how it is. It's better to have loved and lost than to have never loved at all. But I wish I didn't have to lose that love, because I adored her."

"And she loved you. Anyway, a couple of other customers came in, and I need to serve them. You're fine with sitting tight for a moment, right?"

"Yeah. I can do that."

As Lauren ran off, Lisa sighed. She knew her feelings for Anna were there. She was just a bit timid falling in love again. It was all new to her. She hadn't loved another person in the last fifteen years besides Janice. So, she just had to find a way to move forward and to figure out how to love again. That was all she wanted. To love again.

***

That night when Lisa got home, she saw the pictures of Janice in the living room. She knew holding onto the ghosts of the past wasn't good for her. She knew she would either have to tell Anna how she felt, or just leave everything the way it was.

Lisa didn't want to do the latter. She wanted to tell Anna how she felt, even if it killed her.

For the next week, every time Lisa tried to call or text Anna, she held yourself back. That little bit of fear of rejection and denial crept into her thoughts. So, she'd end up stopping herself. "Maybe it's better if I do this after my show," Lisa said.

Lisa felt terrible for putting it off for a week. It had been about a week since she had seen Anna.

Maybe, just maybe, the separation was what she needed, and the best course of action for her. It would better for her to take things with Anna slowly.

Chapter Ten

A few days after she arrived home and settled into her daily routine, Anna finally decided it was time to send a quick text to Lisa.

Anna: Hi, just wanted to say hello. Hope all is well. Let me know how you're doing. By the way, thanks again for a special reunion.

Anna still expected a reply text or possibly a call from Lisa. But she didn't receive a reply.

Anna let another day or so pass and she sent another text to Lisa.

Anna: I hope you're doing well. I would love to hear from you.

Even after the second text, Lisa was silent and Anna received no response. Anna wanted to believe that the lack of communication was due to Lisa's phone service being temporarily unavailable. However, she finally realized that it was because she simple didn't hear from Lisa at all.

Every time Anna thought about calling Lisa herself, she stopped herself. She had reached out and Lisa hadn't responded. It may be fate telling her something.

Anna gave it one more day and sent a final text to Lisa.

Anna: I guess I was wrong. I thought you liked me. But your silence speaks volumes.

***

The night that Anna needed to work the art show, she dropped off Nina at Peter's house. When she got inside, Peter looked at her, motioning for her to come in.

"Is everything all right?" he asked.

"I'm not exactly sure. I feel a little led on," she said.

"What's the matter? I thought things were going better for you?"

"It's a long story if you want to hear it."

"Just because we didn't work out, doesn't mean that I don't want what's best for you. If you need someone to talk to, I'm always here for you," Peter offered.

"I appreciate that. Is Nina off in her room?"

"Yeah. I got her that new video game she wanted," he said.

"Good. I'm glad one of us did. It's so weird how we're so good together as parents, but not as a couple," Anna said.

"Well Anna, you're gay. I remember after you had Nina, you didn't want to have sex anymore. We've been co-parenting for years. We're not a good fit for being lovers, but we are will always be friends," he said.

"Well, do you remember when I said I met someone at the airport while I was trapped there?"

"Yeah. I first thought you were messing with me for a moment when you said that," Peter said.

"Well, I gave her my number, but I haven't heard a word from her. No calls or texts. I wonder if she isn't really interested or perhaps she forgot about me. She seemed distant the moment I mentioned seeing each other when we got back home."

"Is she local?" Peter asked.

"She lives in Ashburn. I 've sent her several texts, but I haven't received any responses. I've thought about calling her, but since she hasn't responded to my texts, perhaps it'll backfire on me," Anna said.

"What if it does? Are you going to stop trying and give up?" Peter asked.

"No. I guess I really want to know if what I'm feeling is correct and whether I'm on the right track," Anna pointed out.

"I'll tell you right now, Anna, you are. You need to give yourself a little more credit. I can tell that you're worried about a future relationship. I understand that. The beginning of any relationship will have its rocky moments. That's just the way things go. If she doesn't feel the same way, then move on. Stop obsessing about it," he said.

"I know what you're telling me is true. I really like her and felt a real connect with her. I'm just scared to find out the truth," Anna remarked.

"Maybe she's got her own demons too. We all have them," Peter pointed out.

"True. I also worry that Nina won't like her. You know how I am with that sort of thing. Nina doesn't even know I'm a lesbian," Anna said.

"You never explained it to her? I figured she already knew. I know at school they've been talking about it. You've heard about that, right?"

Anna tensed. "Damn, I haven't read the newsletters for a while," she said.

"There's your problem. The school is becoming more open-minded about gender and sexuality. They've explained to the kids her age or older about this. They're discussing the topic. Perhaps now is a good time for you to have that talk with her. What's the worst that can happen? Remember that not telling your daughter will only hurt you and any future lovers," he said.

"Will I ever see her again?" Anna asked, sighing.

"Well, if she's local, what's holding you two back? I mean, she's obviously close enough to take the same plane Perhaps, you two can meet up?"

"Maybe Nina's not ready to have someone come into her life," Anna pointed out.

"Anna that isn't on you. I don't think it's fair to you, or to Nina. Be honest about your feelings and explain it as you would to someone who doesn't know. Nina might not get it right away, but kids are pretty quick to learn. They're talking about it more and more. So, it's not like you're introducing some 'spanking new' concept to her either," he said.

"You're right. Thanks, Peter. It's great to have someone to talk to about it. I've been thinking about it a lot," Anna said.

"You have to make the choice for yourself on what to do, Anna. If she's worth the trouble, then, by all means, go for it. Otherwise, maybe it's best if you backed off. But, of course, that's ultimately up to you. Anyway, I'll take care of Nina. I hope the art show goes well," he said.

"Thanks Peter. I appreciate it," she replied.

***

They parted ways, and Anna picked the phone up. She decided to call Lisa after all. Her call went straight to voicemail.

"Are you kidding me?" Anna said, puzzled and starting to become a bit angry.

The one time I try to make an effort to talk to Lisa, and of course, this happens. Anna was frustrated and annoyed with the way everything was transpiring. Maybe it was for the best that Anna spent her time alone, getting her job done and seeing what the future holds.

Chapter Eleven

Lisa saved the texts that Anna had sent her. She wasn't quite sure how to proceed. She wanted to talk to Anna, but she didn't know what to say to her. Lisa went over to the bar to see and speak with Lauren. As she entered and walked up to the bar, Lisa saw Lauren cleaning glasses.

Lisa sat down at the bar. Lauren looked up and saw the look on Lisa's face. Lauren raised her left eyebrow in doubt. Then she smiled.

"You're a bit quiet. What's going on?" Lauren asked.

"Nothing is going on. I'll have the usual," Lisa said.

"Of course you will. What, getting nice and drunk the night before your big show?"

"Ha ha, very funny. I need something to take the damn edge off," Lisa said.

"I don't blame you. It's hard out there," Lauren said.

"You're telling me. What, with all the people looking at my art tomorrow. And, the woman I have a crush on eating away at my feelings. It sucks," Lisa said.

"You still have a crush? You should go for it," Lauren said.

"I know, but—" Lisa said.

"But what? Quit whining and do something about it. I mean, she's obviously interested in you. She probably likes you a lot. Perhaps, there's something bothering her about pursuing a relationship," Lauren said.

"I guess so. Still, I'm bad with relationships and dating," Lisa said.

"You're still focused on Janice. You have to realize that moving on isn't going to be a good thing unless you choose to do it. If you're still obsessing over her, it's only going to hurt you," Lauren pointed out.

"You're right and I hate it when you're right," she said.

"I know you do, but someone needs to state the obvious," Lauren said with a smirk.

Lisa groaned, but she didn't think she'd run into Anna anyway. However, when she finished her drink, she let out a sigh.

"Crap, I've got the art show tomorrow night. I hope at least someone backs me and supports my art. I know they're going to be investors, but I want to believe at least one of them will take pity on my ass," Lisa said with a laugh.

"Oh, you'd be amazed. Some people love the sad artist tale," Lauren said.

Lisa finished her drink, her fourth that night. Afterward, the haze of the alcohol calmed her down. After the last drink, she paid her tab and headed back to continue working on her paintings.

***

After Lisa finished her final commission of the night, she sighed. It was nice, but the emptiness really never went away. *Was it because of what happened with Janice? Or something more?* Lisa didn't know herself, but sometimes she just wished that things could be explained better. That life was easier to understand.

When it was time to get ready for the show, Lisa felt a feeling in her body, one that screamed to her she was in for a surprise.

As Lisa gathered her pieces and brought them in, the curator Dominick nodded.

"Glad to see you're doing well after all this time," he said.

"Eh, been better," Lisa admitted.

"I know. I'm terribly sorry for your loss," Dominick said.

"Thanks. I know it couldn't be prevented. You know how it is," she said.

"Still. My condolences," he added.

He walked away, and for a moment, Lisa wondered if the art show was a good idea. She was famous enough to be known in the art community, and people did know about Janice. They would ask about her, but Lisa hoped it wouldn't be a recurring thing.

Not too long after, Lisa had her first investor. They came over, looked at her work, and then nodded.

"You've really improved, Lisa," the investor said.

"Thank you, sir. I'm happy you think so," she replied.

"I'm sorry about what happened to you and with Janice and all," he said.

"It's fine, sir," she said.

"I understand your troubles, but I hope for you, things do go smoother than ever," he said.

"Right. Thank you," she replied.

After he left, Lisa sighed. She knew they'd give her money, if only out of pity. For now, Lisa wanted nothing more than to forget everything.

After a while, she noticed a head of red hair. Immediately, she looked forward, recognizing it.

Anna? she said to herself.

There was no way Anna was at the art show. Why would she be? It made no sense at all! Then Lisa noticed the person come over. When she did, Lisa stopped.

"Hey," Lisa said.

Anna turned and noticed Lisa standing there. A rush of annoyance flooded through her body, making her wonder why this was happening right then and there. But then, Anna spoke.

"I thought you never wanted to speak to me again since I never received a phone call or an answer to my text messages," she said.

"No, that isn't it at all. I'm so sorry for doing that. I'm just going through a lot right now. I've been thinking about you, though," Lisa said.

"Thinking about me so much that you haven't told me what's going on, or checked up on me after the fact," Anna said.

"I said I'm sorry. I came over here because I wanted to see you and try to explain," Lisa muttered.

Anna nodded. "I'll accept your apology, but that doesn't mean I'm not still angry. How did I know how you felt?" Anna asked.

"Isn't it obvious?" Lisa responded, with a bit of defensiveness in her voice.

"Not based on your actions. I wished things were different between us, but I guess it's just the way things are. I still like you a lot," she said.

"I apologize for getting defensive," Lisa said.

"It's okay. I'm angry with myself for getting mad too," Anna replied.

The silence was awkward. Then, Anna spoke.

"Is there a reason why you were avoiding me? Did I do something wrong?" Anna asked.

"You didn't do anything. It's a personal thing. I would like to make it up to you. We can go out for dinner whenever you're free,," Lisa said.

Anna nodded and said, "That sounds like the start of the perfect apology. Anyway, I can see you put a lot of effort into your artwork. I hope things go well for you."

"Thank you, I truly appreciate that," Lisa said. Lisa felt a flush against her face.

"I'm going to tell my boss, Rupert about you. He said for me to choose someone to give a bit of our funding to. I like your art. So, yeah," Anna said.

"You don't have to do that," Lisa said.

"I want to," Anna insisted.

Lisa nodded. "Fair enough. What do you want from me then," she asked.

"A date," Anna said with a smile.

Lisa looked at her with shock on her face.

"You mean the two of us," Lisa asked.

"Of course, you and I. I want to go on a date with you, Lisa. I know deep down you want that too," Anna said.

Lisa blushed but then nodded. "I'd be lying otherwise," she said.

"Good. I'm glad we see things somewhat similarly. I hope that we can both work through it together," she said.

"I do too," Lisa agreed.

"I should probably head to the other artists. Most of them aren't as exciting as your art though," Anna said.

"Welcome to the art community around here. They usually have the personality of a bunch of sticks. I'm only popular because of a few pieces sold not too long ago. However, I'd rather talk to you more than anything," Lisa said.

"Well, I'm glad I can do something," she said.

"You've done a lot. Thanks," Lisa said.

Anna then turned, looking at Lisa once more before speaking.

"And answer my texts, will you?" Anna teased.

Anna walked off, leaving Lisa standing there and processing everything that just transpired. She was happy to finally have some support, some funding. and some assistance. How should she open up to Anna. Perhaps being a mom, Anna understood the power of loving someone to the point where, even in death, giving up how and what you felt was hard. All Lisa could do was jump and make another leap of faith.

Chapter Twelve

Anna noticed the slight hesitation agreeing to a date. Anna didn't believe it was more than being surprised at the art show, but something seemed almost off.

Still, she couldn't stay angry or upset. Anne understood that everyone had reasons for doing what they did and what they do. Anna was relieved and elated seeing her again. Anna called Peter to give him the news.

"Hey Anna," he said.

"Hi, Peter. I have a date on Sunday with Lisa. Can you take care of Nina?"

"Of course. I wanted to do that anyway. I want to take her ice skating," he said.

"That's perfect. Thanks, Peter," she said.

"Congrats by the way. I'm glad you're finally moving forward in life and not holding yourself back," he said with a laugh.

"I'm trying Peter. I'm still concerned about Nina."

"Anna, I'm her dad, and I'm pretty sure if you told her that you were a three-headed dragon, she wouldn't care. She adores you. She'll understand," he said.

"Thanks Peter," she said.

"No problem. Anyway, it's late and I have work in the morning. Good night," he replied.

Anna hung up and sighed. She was happy to have a date, but she wasn't sure where to take Lisa. As Anna was mulling over places to go on their first date, Lisa texted her. She wanted to take Anna to a pottery class where they could make Christmas items. Anna just assumed they'd do that and maybe go home, but Lisa also said to dress warm. Anna felt a bit relieved. She wondered what Lisa had in store.

Anna made her way to her car after leaving the art show. She drove home thinking about Lisa. Before long, Anna drove up her drive. She was home. She walked into her house and went directly upstairs. She took a bath. While soaking in her tub, she thought about her work schedule.

Tomorrow would be a half-day at work. She would spend time on the projects that needed to be wrapped up. . She hoped everything worked out in her favor.

As she continued with her bath, Anna began to wonder what Lisa was going to do that weekend. She knew that Lisa had a creative bug. She was an artist after all. Anna felt a smile creep up on her face.

She was excited to see where this date would end.

After her bath, Anna went to bed and slept soundly that night.

***

The next day, she went to Lisa's place. After knocking on the door, Lisa showed up in a cute peacoat, her blonde hair pulled back into a nice updo.

"There you are. Ready to go?" she asked.

"Of course. I'm excited," Anna said.

"I am too. This pottery class will be fun," Lisa said.

69

Anna meant the actual time they'd spend together, but she was excited for the class too. Anna and Lisa walked to the car. Anna noticed that Lisa opened the door for her. A real "gentlewoman" if she did say so herself.

"You're so sweet," Anna said.

"It's a pleasure for such a beautiful woman as you," she said with a smile.

Anna flushed, and for a moment, neither of them spoke. Anna then looked at Lisa and sighed.

"I'm just glad you agreed to it. I've been a little worried you'd call it off at the last second," Anna said.

"And what makes you think that?" she teased.

"I don't know. You seem a bit more reserved. It makes me wonder if you regret reconnecting with me," Anna said.

"It isn't regret. It's a long story that I'll share with you soon. I've thought about you a lot. It's strange but meeting you as I did, falling as I did for you and then saying goodbye. Well, I missed you, Anna," she said.

Anna looked at her, trying to see if she was lying, but she wasn't.

"You're telling the truth," Anna pointed out.

"Why wouldn't I be? I know how it is Anna. To think nobody cares or loves you. I know how you felt when I didn't answer you back. It's definitely something I'm not too proud of. You make me happy Anna. You make me happy. There's no real explanation why we ran into each other as we did. Perhaps it could be fate that brought us together.," Lisa said.

Anna sat there, trying to take in all that Lisa said to her. Then she buckled her seatbelt and was ready to go.

Lisa started the car. Anna watched as they sped away, heading over to the pottery studio. The whole date felt almost surreal. She still had that little bit of doubt in the back of her mind. However, she knew that Lisa was being honest with her. There was something powerful and refreshing with doing that.

When they arrived at the studio, Lisa parked near the front. Then they proceeded to walk inside. They were signed up for a beginner's couple class. When they sat down in the corner, Anna sighed.

"It feels nice to be in a place where people encourage you to create. I don't really do much creation at my day job," Anna said.

"You're an investor," Lisa said.

"That's a nice way to put it. Basically, I just tally up a bunch of bullshit, write down some numbers, and then go on my merry way," Anna said.

"Sounds rough," Lisa said.

"I'm trying the best I can. It's not easy out there," Anna said.

"You're telling me. There's a lot that I'd like to tell you about. A lot of it would help explain everything," she said.

"I know you have your own demons. And, I don't want to pry," Anna said.

"I'm sorry for not telling you sooner either. Things are hard for me. Hard to explain. I have a lot of baggage. That's partially why I was so distant about talking to you because I didn't know how you'd take it.

But you deserve an explanation Anna, which I'll give you later," she said.

"Thanks, Lisa. I know that, even with how things have been, talking to you now makes everything better," Anna said.

"Talking to you has done me a lot of good. I welcome the conversation," she said.

"I welcome it too," Anna replied.

For a moment, they didn't say anything more. Anna could see the true colors coming out of Lisa's words. The truth about what was happening. Lisa was a broken woman. She was suffering in her own way. She had a difficult time talking about it, even to Anna. However, Anna understood why.

She could see Lisa was struggling with everything that was happening to her. Anna felt the pain that she was going through. Anna just wanted to sit there and tell her it would be okay, even when she doubted that herself.

***

After the pottery class was done, Anna then held Lisa's hand. Lisa felt a blush creep up on her cheeks.

"Sorry if it's awkward or anything," Anna said.

"No, it's wonderful. There are Christmas lights in the park. I'd love to take you there," she said.

Anna nodded. "I'd love that too," she replied.

They took each other's hands. For a moment, neither own said anything. It was obvious Anna was definitely nervous, but she could see that Lisa was just as nervous. As they made their way over to the car, Anna wanted to ask what happened, why the sudden change, and that she understood the issues going on.

Anna left it at that. She knew that Lisa would speak when she was ready.

"Don't worry about me, Anna. I'm fine," she said.

"You say that, but I can tell you're not," Anna said.

"I am, Anna. I'll tell you everything that's going on, I promise," she replied.

Anna nodded, wondering herself what was happening. They climbed into the car and drove to the park.

***

"We're here," Lisa said.

Anna got out, looked at Lisa for a second, and then back at the place around her. It was beautiful. Anna gasped at the sight of the breathtaking beauty. There were lights all around. Even though she normally didn't feel the Christmas spirit, there was something about the park that made it trickle in.

"It's wonderful," Anna said.

"It sure is," Lisa said.

"I'm so happy right now," Anna said.

"I am too. I'm glad I got to share it with you. I've wanted to come here for a while. But I felt a little bit limited since I didn't have anyone to go with," she said.

"Well, we came together," Anna said.

"Perfect," she said.

Anna then looked at her. Lisa seemed fine, but Anna could also see the downcast look to her eyes.

Something upset her, but she doesn't know what.

The time they spent together was wonderful. They explored all of the different paths, all the lights and sounds that were there. It certainly was a different experience. Anna started to feel the way things were and the difference it made in her life. Then, Anna pointed to a bench. There was a hot cocoa station nearby. Lisa went over to get some. Anna sat down, shivering slightly. When Lisa returned with hot cocoa, they sat together.

"I want to get a picture of this, if that's okay?" Lisa asked.

"Sure, why wouldn't it be?" Anna inquired.

"I'm sorry. It's just a bad habit of asking," she said.

"You're fine. You don't have to ask," Anna said.

They took the picture together, both of them sitting pleasantly and smiling. When Lisa was finished, she turned to Anna.

"Send that to me, please," Anna asked.

"Sure. Here," Lisa said.

The image was quickly sent, and Anna looked at it, smiling.

"You're the first woman I've gone out with who does things like that. It's cute," Lisa said.

"Well, you matter a lot to me, Anna. And I think it's time you heard the explanation behind my aloofness," she said.

Anna nodded, sat there and was ready to listen. Whatever Lisa had to tell her was something they needed to discuss. Something important.

Chapter Thirteen

Lisa sighed, knowing that whatever she said next could determine their future. She sighed and began to speak.

"So, to preface all of this, this is something from my past that I need to discuss with you," she said.

"Okay. That's fine," Anna replied.

"The truth is, I lost my former partner about two years ago. She had cancer," Lisa said.

"I'm so sorry to learn that," Anna said.

"Thanks for that. I've been looking to move on. You've helped me start to do that, Anna. The story behind her is simple. When I was younger, I met this woman. Her name was Janice. I loved her a lot. We spent fifteen years together, but we never married. She had issues with her body, especially when it came to endometriosis. However, neither one of us believed it would turn what it did," she explained.

"What happened?" Anna asked.

"Cervical cancer. It came on so suddenly. She always had her pap smears, always saw her doctor. One day, it just grew. It turned out that she was so far gone that when she died, she was already in terrible shape. They tried to do chemo, but it was too much for her body. They tried to remove the cancer, but it was a pretty traumatic situation for both of us. I stayed by her side every step of the journey because I loved her. I was with her until the day she passed. I followed her wishes and cremated her. I've felt empty ever since. I always felt like we'd be the couple who grew old together. It wasn't the case. Instead, it was the harsh reality that people do die, that life does end at death, and it sucks," she said.

"I'm so sorry," Anna said.

"Don't be. She's in a better place. Before she passed, she said if I ever found someone who made me feel the same way as I did for her, I needed to follow my heart. I needed to fall in love and never let her go. She wanted me to be happy. Her last words have hung with me all this time. Anna, I want to be happy. I really do," she said.

"I want you to be happy," Anna said.

"The reason why I didn't say anything is that I was scared. I didn't know if you'd run away knowing my tale. I was afraid to face my feelings and come to terms with it all. After a lot of soul-searching and thinking, I have a better understanding of who I am. I know what I want now. Anna, I want you. I've fallen in love with you," Lisa said.

Anna looked at her with surprise.

"You do?" she asked.

"I do. Why, is that bad?" she asked.

"Not at all. I love you too Lisa. I really do. The concept of love is strange to me. I thought I loved Peter, but it just wasn't for me. With you, I feel like all of the worry, all of the fear, and all of the pain from the past is gone. I can look forward to a future," she said.

"I'm sorry for not being honest sooner. Things are sometimes hard. I still have a bit of work to do to recover. I've never experienced death the way I did when I lost her completely. It's a hard road, but it's a road I'm working to travel on better," she said.

"And you're doing great," Anna said.

"Thank you. I do appreciate the support," she said with a smile.

Lisa felt happy and excited. Despite all of the struggles in the past, everything seemed real.

"By the way Lisa, I do want to apologize. For pushing you so much. I'm sorry if I got mad when we met up at the art gallery. I didn't mean to sound so angry. I was just concerned and saddened to think you had forgotten about me, or you didn't care. I now understand why," she said.

"Death affects us all differently. I know with myself, it's hard to let go of certain feelings. You're a strong woman, and I do applaud everything you do," she said.

.

The smile that was on Anna's face warmed Lisa's heart. She didn't regret telling Anna and sharing her feelings. Everything felt right and so real.

It was obvious that it was the beginning of something, something that even Lisa didn't understand herself. However, the unknown wasn't going to get in the way. Lisa was just happy to finally start making progress, to finally move on, and finally feel whole once more.

"Do you want to see each other?" Anna asked.

"Of course. And when the time is right, I'll meet Nina," she said.

"Good. I want you to. I've been worried about Nina because I don't know how she'll take it," Anna said.

"She's ten, right? She should at least understand what's going on. You know, with people being in love and all," Lisa explained.

"You'd be surprised. I'm not sure how kids take this stuff these days. I want to believe it'll be all right," she said.

"Anna, if I can start to come to terms with my past, you can tell her. I'm sure she's old enough to understand," Lisa said.

"I know she is. That's not the part I'm worried about. I'm worried she won't accept it," she said.

"I know Anna. But, you're not going through any of this alone. I'll help you and you help me heal and move on. I know you make me happy. I don't have sex with just anyone. But I guess, the right person makes me feel like it's worth it. Anna, you're the right one to me," she said.

"I felt the same way. I don't know if 'fate' was at work there or not. But, I'm happy to be by your side, Lisa. Happy to have you here with and beside me," she said.

"I'm glad you understand Anna," Lisa said.

The kiss they shared at that point made Lisa's heart lurch. She loved Anna. Lisa knew that, no matter what the odds, no matter what may happen next, everything would be okay. It was the beginning of a brighter, better future. It was Anna's beginning too.

When they pulled away from their kiss, Anna flushed.

"I'm glad you're here. I'll try to talk to Nina about everything as quickly as I can," she said.

"Don't rush it. Take all the time you feel you need. I'll be here regardless," she said.

"My ex-husband, Peter, invited me to Christmas dinner. He said I could bring you. I know it might be awkward, but I think he wants to meet you because he thinks of you as becoming a part of the family. Are you okay with that?" Anna asked.

Lisa blushed. She didn't think she was worth that much. But she was happy to at least be acknowledged by Anna's family.

"Let me think about it and I'll get right back with you," Lisa said.

"Good. Thank you, Lisa," she said.

"Anyway, let's head on back," Lisa said.

They made their way to the car, sighing in relief at the warm air as it hit them. When they drove back, neither of them said much, their minds on other things. Lisa knew that no matter what happened and no matter what life threw at Anna or herself, everything would be fine.

***

When they arrived at Lisa's place. Anna and Lisa said their goodbyes.

"I should be going. I've got Nina all next week, but if you want, we can spend time together in between me working and then heading home. Though, I might be busy with the new projects too," she said.

"Okay. I have my own projects to worry about," she said.

Anna bade farewell before heading out. Lisa watched her drive away and disappear in the distance. She let out a long sigh. *I want to let go of these feelings. To finally move on, after all this time, she told herself.*

Lisa entered her home and shut the door behind her. She saw all the pictures of her and Janice. The pictures with them smiling, with them both feeling happy and loved by each other, the pictures of a different time. Anna was different from Janice. While Lisa loved and did love Janice, she knew Anna was her chance for a new life. Lisa wanted nothing more than to just let things go the way she wanted them to.

Perhaps it was also one of the reasons why she hadn't moved on. She was holding onto those memories instead of letting go.

Lisa grabbed each of the pictures. She looked at them and remembered the happy memories with Janice. Then she gave each one a final kiss goodbye. She would finally leave that part of her past, and finally, move onto the future.

"I'm sorry Janice, but I've found someone new. You told me it was time to move on. I'm going to do just that. Move on," she said.

She took the pictures and put them in the box that she had on hand. She took them, putting them in the storage room she never visited. They say out of sight, out of mind, but there was no way Lisa could ever forget Janice.

For the first time in a long time, Lisa was happy. She knew that Anna loved her, and the future they had together was real. She was no longer going to allow the memories of her past to hold her back. Instead, she would onto her memories because they were a part of her life. They would no longer hold her back from life.

Lisa now felt safe, secure and ready for the future. She was happy. It was the beginning of a bright, rewarding future. Lisa also felt her relationship with Anna was just the beginning of things to come. However, she also thought it would be best to take things slowly, to see where it would go, and to go from there.

At least, that was what she thought.

***

An hour or so passed when Lisa decided she needed to call Anna. For a moment, she heard a pause, and then Anna spoke.

"Hi Lisa. Is everything okay?" she asked.

"Yes. I wanted you to know that I accept your invitation to dinner for Christmas. I'm doing a whole lot better, and I'm ready to be the best person I can be for you," she said.

There was a chuckle on the other end of the line. While Lisa didn't understand what was so funny, she could tell Anna was definitely in a better mood herself.

"I'm glad you finally worked through it. This is the beginning of a new life for the both of us," Anna said.

"It sure is. It's time to move on. It's time to have the best experience possible. I'm ready to take a chance again, no matter what," Lisa said.

Anna giggled. Lisa felt her heart becoming whole. She knew that it was the future she decided for herself. No matter what life threw at her next, everything would be okay.

Chapter Fourteen

Anna had just arrived home when she received an urgent call from the emergency department at Monroe General Hospital. Anna picked up her phone and didn't recognize the number. However, something told her to answer it.

"Hello?" Anna asked.

"May I speak to Ms. Anna Jackson, please," the unknown voice asked.

"This is she. And you are?" Anna asked.

"This is Gloria at Monroe General Hospital. A Peter Jackson was brought to the emergency room about an hour ago after suffering a serious fall."

"Oh Jesus," Anna said. Peter wasn't that old, but he was a little clumsy. She knew he probably fell and hurt his back or something.

"We wanted to let you know that he's here. You are on his emergency contact list to call."

"Is my daughter in there as well?" she asked.

"Yes, she's here and being watched by one of the nurses. You daughter is a brave girl. She called 911."

"How is Peter doing?" Anna asked.

"He is currently with the doctors. His status is unknown at this time. As soon as you arrive at the hospital, go straight to the emergency ward. You can speak with the doctors at that time."

"Thank God. Can you tell me how my daughter is handling it? she asked.

"From what I've heard, she's just a little shaken up by everything," the hospital worker said.

"I don't blame her. I'm sure it scared her. Thank you so much. I'm on my way," Anna said.

Racing over to the hospital, Anna felt like her heart was beating a 100 times an minute. Her heart raced. While she was no longer with Peter, she knew about his bad back. This wasn't going to be fun for anyone.

When she got to the hospital, she ran inside, motioning to the nurses to find out where he was. She got to the room. There was Nina, with one of the hospital nurses, holding her hand.

"Your dad will be okay sweetie," the nurse said.

"Hey. I'm her mom. Is Peter all right?" Anna asked.

Anna looked at the nurse, who then pulled her to the side. Anna followed. When she got over there, the nurse spoke.

"There is a problem," she said.

"What do you mean?"

"When Peter fell, he fell on some sort of object and injured himself. He has several deep wounds. He may have some internal bleeding as well. The doctors are trying to stabilize him now. Depending on what the doctors find, there is always the possibility that he may not make it through," she said.

"Oh God," Anna said.

"I haven't been able to tell your daughter yet, but you should definitely have that conversation with her," the nurse said.

Anna had a lot of explaining to do.

"I will. Thank you for taking care of her. I was with a friend. I need to call them too," Anna said.

"Boyfriend?"

"Girlfriend," Anna replied.

"I see. Your daughter will need you now more than ever. If he does survive, he could be facing a long recovery," she said.

"All right," Anna replied.

Anna went over to Nina, looking at her and smiling.

"Hey, sweetie. There is something Mommy needs to tell you," she said.

"What is it?" she asked.

"Let's talk outside," she said.

Anna wasn't sure how to break the news to Nina, but she knew that Nina needed someone, anyone who could tell her what was going on. Anna walked over to the small sitting area where a couple of heaters were. It was a little chilly, but not terrible outside. Not like the airport, she was in just a couple weeks ago.

Anna sat down, motioning for Nina to sit down next to her. Anna took a deep breath, looking at Nina for but a moment before speaking.

"Nina, there is something I need to tell you. Something important," she said.

"What do you mean?" she asked.

"It's about Mommy. So, do you know about what Mommy's been up to?"

"You've been happier I noticed," she said.

"Correct. Well, I met someone. A woman," she said.

"Really? That's awesome!" Nina cried out.

Anna immediately looked at her with a surprised glance.

"You're not upset Mommy kept this from you?"

"You're happy Mommy. I want to meet her. I know you haven't seen anyone since you and Daddy stopped being together, but you look better. You look happy Mom," she said.

"Good. I'm glad you understand. I know the kids in your school were learning about men and women being together with other men and women, and I think that I needed to have this conversation with you," she said.

"Well, I understand Mommy. I learned that girls can be together with girls, and boys can be with boys. And I understand that. If you're happy, I'm happy. Does Daddy know?"

"Daddy offered to have her come to his place for Christmas, but that may change," she said.

"Is Daddy going to be okay?"

"I don't know sweetie. We'll just have to wait and see what the doctors tell us," she said.

Anna was just being honest here. She knew that, if she told Nina anything further, it might scare her. But Nina nodded.

"I hope Daddy gets okay and gets better," she said.

"So do I, honey. So do I," Anna said.

Anna was trying her hardest to make it easier for Nina, even if things weren't all that easy to explain. After a minute, she heard the sound of pattering footsteps, and when she looked up, one of the nurses was there.

"We wanted to let you know there was a change. Surprisingly, he's stabilizing. He is about to go into surgery. We're going to have to ask you to leave after you say your goodbyes. You can wait in the patient lounge, she said.

"Got it. Thank you," Anna said.

Anna got up and grasped Nina's hand.

"Let's go see him," she said.

Anna walked to Peter's room, with Nina's hand in her own. She was happy her daughter was at least listening to her. Things weren't easy for either of them. She was just trying her best. When she got inside, she saw him there, a tear fell down her face.

"All right let's get this over with," Anna said.

She sat down at the chair next to the bed, holding Peter's hand.

"Peter, I want you to pull through. Your daughter and I want to all see you again," she said.

"Yes, Daddy. I want to spend Christmas with you," Nina said.

There was a small change in the heart rate, which surprised even Anna, but then, she sighed.

"He might be listening. Not totally sure," Anna said.

"I think he is," one of the nurses said.

"I'll take care of her, Peter. I want you to stick around too," she said.

Anna then sighed, moving away. Nina then grasped his hand.

"Daddy, you'll come back. I know you will. I love you to the moon and back," she said.

Anna led Nina out of the room. She was trying her best to hold it all together. She had faith in what would happen next. She had faith in his body and in a speedy recovery. She had faith in everyone.

When Anna made her way over to the lounge with Nina, she picked up her phone She called Lisa.

"Hey, Anna," Lisa said.

"Hi. I wanted you to know that I'm at the hospital. Peter took a bad fall. He's about to go into surgery," she said.

"Do you want me to come on over?" Lisa asked.

"If you want. Or if you want to, we can all meet up first thing tomorrow. I'll have Nina with me. I don't know what's going to happen now. But, I do know that with the way things are, I'm going to have to stay with him," she said.

"It's okay. Does he have any other family?"

"Other than his mom, no. His mother and I aren't on the best of terms. So, I'm going to have to have that conversation with her later," Anna said

"I don't have a lot of experience with children, but if you need anything, Anna, let me know," Lisa said

"Thanks, I appreciate that," Anna replied.

After hanging up the phone, Anna sighed. It would be a long night tonight. She wondered if he'd make it through. She wanted to believe that they would make it, all of them. Anna feared the worst. Her heart raced just thinking about it. She needed to stay in the right mindset, at least for now. She needed to pretend everything was okay, even if, deep down, she wanted to just leave everything and never worry about it again.

The rest of the night was spent sitting around, waiting for any news at all on his condition. She feared the unknown but left it to fate. She hoped that, if he did survive, it wouldn't take him a long time to recover.

Chapter Fifteen

Lisa felt the worry in Anna's voice as she heard the news. Dealing with the death of a loved one wasn't easy. The fact that he may not make it through the night also frightened Anna. Lisa had to stay strong, no matter what happened.

Lisa then looked over at the clock. It was still early enough to go to the bar, and then maybe go to the hospital. Anna said she'd be there for a little while. Lisa then made her way over to her favorite bar, headed to the counter and sighed.

"There you are. Haven't' seen you for a while," Lauren said.

"Hey, Lauren. Sorry, been busy with things," she said.

"What kinds of things?" Lauren asked.

"Just life. Like with the way things are and such," she said.

"Did something happen with Anna?"

"Yeah. Turns out her ex is in the hospital. I'm worried, but I fear going over there. It reminds me of Janice a bit. But, is it really my place?"

"That's for you to decide, Lisa. Do you think you can help her?"

Lisa nodded. "I think I can, but who knows," she said.

"You know how it is. I can tell that you're worried about her, and that, whatever's going through your head is something that you're struggling to come to terms with," she said.

"I know that. What will happen to Anna and me? I mean, I don't fear meeting her ex. However, at the same time, I worry that it might make things awkward if I'm there," Lisa admitted.

"That is something you need to decide for yourself, Lisa. I'm not the boss of what you do, or what you choose. You need to figure out what's best for you. Do you care enough about Anna to step forward, help her make the transition easy, and be there for her? Are you?" Lauren asked.

"Honesty, I'm not sure," Lisa said.

"Well, I don't have any answer to give you," she pointed out.

"You've been helpful, Lauren. A great friend," she said.

" I only want what's best for you in life," she said.

"Thanks," Lisa said.

"You should go see her. It's only right. If she needs your support and help, you need to give it to her," she said.

***

Lisa made her way to the hospital after having her conversation with Lauren. As much as she hated the hospital, it was important to be by Anna's side.

"When Lisa arrived at the hospital, she rushed inside. When she got there, she saw Anna in one of the waiting rooms. When they locked eyes, for a moment Anna didn't say anything.

"How did you—"

"It's not that hard to figure out where you were, Anna," she said.

"I guess this is where you'll meet her," Anna said.

Anna then motioned for Nina to come forward. She looked like Anna in a sense, but different. She must have her father's eyes and nose, but Anna's bright red hair. She was a cute kid. However, Lisa wasn't sure if she was ready for this just yet.

"So, you're Nina?" Lisa said.

"Hi," Nina answered.

"I'm Lisa. I'm your mother's friend. You know about how girls can be with girls. like kissing and such?" Lisa asked.

"I learned about it in school," she said.

"Well, there you go. That's what we are, Nina. I'm your mom's girlfriend, and I won't be leaving her side through any of this," she said.

"It's nice to meet you," Nina replied.

"It's a pleasure to meet you, too," Lisa said with a smile.

Anna didn't really know how Nina would take the news. For a moment, as Nina went over to play with some of the toys, Anna didn't say anything.

"So, you came to see me," Anna said.

"I only want what's best for you Anna," she said.

"Well, it's appreciated. Thanks Lisa," she said.

"You're welcome. Being here for you and your daughter is my way of showing how much I care," she said.

"It's really nice of you," Anna said.

"I know it's not an easy subject to deal with, but I hope Peter makes it through. Because I want to meet him," Lisa said.

"You seem different. You're not as distant anymore," she said.

Lisa paused. She didn't think it was that obvious. Judging from the way that Anna was looking at her, there was something there.

"Let's just say that I learned the value of being there for the people you love, and moving on," she said.

"In a sense, you're now part of the family," she said.

"Well, I'm honored to be a part of your family, Anna," she said.

"Good. I want that Lisa. I really do," she replied.

"Me too," Lisa said with a smile on her face.

The moment Lisa uttered those words, Anna realized that this was her home, her future and she was happy. For the first time, she really was.

They sat down in the waiting area, hoping the answers would be provided soon. After what seemed to be forever, someone came out. When Lisa looked at the person, she noticed it was a doctor. However, they weren't somber. They were instead, looking at them with almost a relieved glance.

"You're Peter's ex-wife, correct?" they said.

"Yes, I am," Anna replied.

"Peter came through it will no complications. In fact, his injuries could have been worse. Thankfully, his internal bleeding was isolated to a small region on the right side of his body. He did exacerbate his herniated disc, but thankfully it didn't rupture. He's still sedated and currently in recovery," the doctor said.

Anna looked relieved, and so did Lisa. She felt relieved for Anna because she knew how these situations could turn out. It was obvious that it was only going to get easier for them from there.

"As I said, Peter is in recovery. So, give some time and we'll take you back. Wait here. As soon as he's awake, we'll let you know," the surgeon said.

Anna thanked the doctor as he turned around to return to recovery. As he passed by Nina, he touched the top of her head and gave her a wink.

***

Anna, Nina and Lisa sat in the recovery waiting room anticipating Peter's recovery and when they could see him. Time seemed to pass so slowly. Before long, one of the nurses came into the waiting room and went up to Anna.

"Peter is comfortable and awake. Would you like to go inside?" the nurse asked.

"I'd love that," Anna said.

"Do you want me to come in?" Lisa said.

Anna nodded.

"Yes. You came to support me and my daughter, so it's only fair," she said with a grin.

Lisa flushed, but then, she headed inside. When they got there, Anna looked at Peter, smiling.

"Hi, Peter," Anna said.

"Hello," he said weakly.

"This is Lisa," Anna said.

Lisa nervously stepped forward, wondering what he would say. He then extended his hand, nodding.

"I'm Peter. Nice to meet you. Take care of Anna and Nina," he said.

"I will," Lisa replied.

"You need to sleep and get some rest," the doctor said.

"Yes, he does," Anna replied.

Peter fell quickly to sleep. Lisa felt happy and safe. She knew Anna was serious about them being together and was happy to have her around. For Lisa, that alone was enough to make her feel welcomed and loved. Lisa knew for a fact that things would get better with time.

Chapter Sixteen

For Anna, the whole emergency situation was enough to make her want to sleep for fifty years, but she had Nina to deal with too. While she did love her daughter, she knew Nina was struggling herself. When Nina started to look around the room, and then at her father, she spoke.

"Is Daddy really okay?" she asked.

"Yes, sweetie. Daddy will be okay," she said.

"All right. Thanks, Mommy," Nina said.

After Anna finished at the hospital, she took Nina home. Lisa followed after. She planned on staying with Anna and Nina. Anna really appreciated everything Lisa did.

"Are you sure it's okay Lisa? I know you have a busy day of work tomorrow," Anna said.

"It's fine," Lisa said.

"Okay. I Love you," Anna said.

Saying "I love you" made Anna realize that she did mean it. She did love Lisa, even if things weren't perfect. Lisa smiled back at her, and for Anna, she knew for a fact that even when things weren't easy, it would all be fine.

Nina also seemed happy about it. When Anna got back home, she quickly made a call to her office, leaving a message to let them know what was going on. She also told them that she planned on coming in later on. She just needed some sleep, and to think about the next part of this. For Anna, she was just happy that at least Peter would be okay.

Nina went to bed, tired from everything that happened. Anna wanted to sleep too, but she felt that there were still things that needed to be discussed.

"So, are you doing okay?" Lisa asked.

"I've been better. And yourself?"

"Same. I'm worried about you. You're trying your best to keep everything together, but you're struggling. I can see it," Lisa said.

"I still worry about Peter. He's certainly a good man and damn good father. There's a lot that needs to be done," Anna said.

"You're an amazing woman, and a good mom. Your daughter means the world to you. I can tell that with everything going on, it's not easy for you, but you're doing the best you can," Lisa said.

"Thanks, Lisa. I really am. I don't understand why it's so hard for me, but I do feel like, with the way everything is, it's not an easy task for me to achieve, but I'm trying my best," Anna said.

"Well, you're supermom to me. I always thought that it would get easier. It isn't. But, at least this time around I'm not alone," Lisa said to her.

"You're right. you're not alone. You have me. And, I have you," Anna said.

For a moment, neither of them said much else, unsure of what to. Then, Anna leaned in, giving Lisa a deep, loving kiss. Lisa kissed her back. Together, they shared the feeling of pleasure that they had with each other.

The kiss they shared was different this time around. It wasn't just an average kiss, one that would prove to be only worse with wear. Instead, it was one that proved to be loving and proved to be something that was deep and amazing with each other. For Lisa, she felt they would be okay.

When Anna pulled away, she reddened.

"Sorry," Anna said.

"For what," Lisa asked.

"For everything," Anna told Lisa.

"What do you mean by that?" Lisa asked.

"With my child, with everything that has happened. I feel a little guilty," she admitted.

"You're totally fine, Anna," Lisa admitted.

"I know you say that, but I'm overwhelmed and worried," she said.

"I know you are. And, you have full right to worry. But, try not to. I'm not leaving you alone, Anna. I promise," she stated to Anna.

"I do hope that Peter pulls through. I appreciate all that you've done for me," she said.

Lisa nodded and hugged Anna.

"I think we should go to bed. You're more than welcomed to stay. Peter should be more awake tomorrow, from what the doctors said," Anna said.

"It's all going to be fine. We've got this," Lisa replied.

Anna gave her another long, passionate kiss. Everything just felt so right with Lisa. Maybe it was just how things should be. Anna then, after all that, headed to bed, with Lisa following suit. Neither of them knew where the future would take them, but Anna knew one thing for sure. With Lisa, everything felt right, and she didn't have to worry anymore.

It was a different feeling, but she wouldn't complain.

Chapter Seventeen

Lisa woke up the next morning to someone holding her hand. She looked, and for a moment, her brain almost went to Janice. Then, she looked and realized that it wasn't her.

It was Anna. A warm feeling of love coursed through Lisa's body. After Anna started to stir, Lisa then looked down at her, smiling.

"Did you sleep okay?" Lisa asked.

"Yes, I certainly did. We should probably get up. Nina doesn't have school, but I've got work later on. I may go see Peter beforehand," she said.

"Don't worry about it. I'll take care of Nina," Lisa said.

"Are you sure? I mean, she's not your child. I don't want to—"

"I'm okay with it," she said.

"All right," Anna said.

When they got up, Anna bade Nina and Lisa farewell, heading out the door. Lisa looked at Nina, who was slightly nervous.

"I'm not going to hurt you," she said.

"I know, I'm just surprised," Nina said.

"About what?"

"About Mommy falling in love again. I thought she loved Daddy, but that wasn't real love. They were both upset about things, but I never asked why," Nina said.

"It can be hard for a child to get it. But, if you ever need anything, I'm here for you. I won't replace your dad, but I'm here to make your life as good as it can be," Lisa said.

Nina grinned. Lisa felt a small feeling of hope course through her veins as she saw the little kid smile. *Maybe this was it. Maybe this was what she needed.*

"What would you like to do today, Nina? I'll be taking care of you until your mother gets home," she said.

"I wouldn't mind getting Mommy a gift," she said.

"That's a wonderful idea! We can go together," Lisa said.

"Did Mommy leave you with money though?" Nina asked.

"Nope, but we can make it work," Lisa explained.

Nina looked at her with confusion. Then, Lisa smiled.

"It'll be our little secret. You can give Mommy an amazing gift. And maybe, we'll get one for Daddy too," Lisa said.

There was something about helping Nina out that warmed her heart. Suddenly, Nina looked at her with widened eyes.

"I have the perfect gift for Mommy," she said.

"Sure, let's get it then," Lisa said.

Lisa took Nina's hand, headed over to the car and then drove to the mall. Nina ran toward the doorway. Lisa followed suit, curious as to what the Nina wanted to buy. When they got inside, she rushed toward one of the clothing stores, inciting Lisa's curiosity as she walked in.

The walls were lined with different items, trinkets and such which piqued her curiosity. Then, Lisa noticed Nina walk over to the cabinet, pointing at a turquoise pendant.

"Here. Get this for Mommy. Say it's from me. It's her favorite color," she said.

Lisa looked at the item, noticing that it was a beautiful bright blue tone. It would complement her hair very well.

"Well, that works perfectly for your gift. What about me though".

"You should give her a picture. She'd like that," Nina said.

"I think that's a good idea!" she said, smiling at the thought.

Lisa had a feeling a painting would be perfect for her. The holiday season didn't just have to be material gifts. Sentimental gifts worked too.

"Sure, but of what?"

"Maybe you, me and her? She would enjoy that. I know she loves art. I remember one time she gave Daddy this pretty picture. While he liked it, she enjoyed it a lot more," Nina explained.

"Well, I'll do that then," Lisa said.

She thought about what to paint her, what to give her to make it worth her while. But then, Nina smiled again, and Anna grew curious once more.

"What's the matter?"'

"Oh, just thinking about the look on Mommy's face when she gets the painting," she said.

"I figured as much. Does your mom really like paintings?"

"Yes. She always wanted to date an artist," Nina explained.

"Well, she clearly found the one then," Lisa said with a laugh.

"Do you think you're going to get married?" Nina asked.

Lisa paused. As much as she liked Anna, she wasn't sure about that yet. She knew that, with Anna, things could be different, but she wouldn't mind.

"Maybe down the road, but not just yet," she said.

"Okay. Just asking," Nina said.

Lisa laughed. The kid understood a lot more than she let on. After they made the purchase, Lisa and Nina both went back to the house. Lisa then sighed.

"I'll start painting it after your mom gets back. For now, do you want to make some ornaments." Lisa said.

"Sure!" Anna said.

Lisa smiled, showing Anna how to make some homemade Christmas ornaments. The happiness Lisa felt when she spent time with Nina warmed her heart, making her wonder if there was a reason for it. She had a feeling that, with Anna, things would only go up from there, and things would get easier with time.

Anna arrived home about four hours later. When she saw Lisa and Nina on the couch, she smiled.

"You two look comfy," she pointed out.

"Yeah, we are. Nina and I have talked a lot today. We've been hanging out."

"Yeah, and we even got Christmas gifts!" Nina said.

"How fun! I'm excited to see what you got me," Anna said.

"Well, I would like to give yours to you the night before. Not in front of everyone, if that's okay," Lisa said.

"Sure. It's nothing like *that* is it?" Anna asked.

"Oh, not at all! It's just something I'd prefer to give to you in private," she said.

Anna nodded. "I can't wait," she said.

"Good. Anyway, I need to head back to my place after dinner. I'm going to work on your present tonight," Lisa said with a smile.

Anna then looked at her. For a moment, the beaming smile warmed Lisa's heart. It felt so right, so real. Lisa couldn't wait to see what Anna would think about her gift.

She hoped Anna loved it.

Chapter Eighteen

Anna was curious about the gift Lisa was going to give to her, but she stopped herself from asking. It was something she'd learn about eventually when Lisa felt that it was time. For now, she was just happy that Lisa was here with her, happy and satisfied.

After work over the next few days, they spent time together. Anna noticed that Lisa was leaving earlier, probably to go work on the gift. Anna felt happy, but then, she noticed Nina looking at her.

"Something the matter, sweetie?"

"No Mom, I just noticed you're happy," she said.

"I am. I really am, honey. Lisa has helped me a lot," Anna said.

"Good Mom," she said.

"Do you like her too? I wouldn't want to do anything you wouldn't like," Anna said.

"No, I love her Mommy," Nina said.

Anna smiled, feeling happy and amazed at how well life was going. It was only a few days until Christmas, and Anna was excited.

"We should go see your father tonight," she said.

"Okay Mommy," Nina said.

***

Anna and Nina drove over to the hospital. As they walked to the entrance, Anna smiled at her daughter. Nina was holding her hand a little bit. Anna felt good about her family. They entered the hospital and made their way to his room.

"Hi, Peter," Anna said.

"Hi, Anna. Hey, sweetie," Peter said, lightly petting Nina's head.

"Hey Daddy," she said with a grin.

"You feeling better?" Anna asked.

"Define better," he said with a smile.

"You know what I mean," Anna said.

"Like I'm alive and don't feel like death? Yeah, I feel much better," he said cheerfully.

"Well good. You had me worried for a moment," Anna admitted.

"That makes two of us. I don't know how I managed to live to tell the tale myself," he said.

"Luck, and a good surgeon," Anna said.

"Yeah, mostly just that. Anyway, I think I vaguely met Lisa. Are things good for you two?" he asked.

"We're doing better," she said.

"Good. I'm happy for you two. From what I can remember, she seemed like a fine woman," he admitted.

"Yes, she is," she replied.

"Good. Now I don't need to worry about you," he said.

"You don't, but I thank you for your concern," Anna said with a smile on her face.

"You're most welcome. I know how it can be" he said.

"You're telling me. I'm happy" Anna said.

"Is she still coming over for Christmas? I know my mom will probably have to come over to at least help me with tasks around the house, but I think she'll leave afterward. She understands that I just need a little help right now," he said.

"Yeah. That'll work," she said.

"Perfect. Can't wait to see you. I can take Nina too starting tomorrow night. Since it's Christmas eve," Peter said.

"It is? I didn't even realize that," she admitted.

"It's okay. It's been a rough few weeks, but it's finally ending sooner rather than later," he said.

"You've got that right," Anna laughed.

"If you want to spend some time alone with her, go for it. I'll gladly help you as much as I can," he said.

"Thanks, Peter. You're so good to me," she said.

"It's because I know how it can be. How it can affect all of us," he said.

Anna nodded, blushing.

"That's true," she said.

***

After Peter was released from the hospital and arrived home, Anna dropped off Nina and then went back to the house again, sighing in happiness.

While she was happy about the fact that things were going better between Peter and her, she wondered what Lisa was up to. For the first time since they got together, she realized Lisa wasn't answering her texts, which bothered Anna slightly.

She wondered what Lisa was up to. *Oh well, they'd be meeting for dinner tomorrow anyway. No sense in getting hung up on that.* Still, Anna did have a few doubts in her mind, but it was better not to worry about things.

The next evening, Anna heard a doorbell ring. Anna walked on over, and when she opened it, she saw Lisa standing there. She had bags under her eyes and looked tired, but a beaming grin was present on her face.

"Hello," Lisa said.

"Hello yourself. What's all this?" Anna asked.

"Oh, this? I brought it over for you. It's your gift," she said.

Anna looked at it with surprise. Then, Lisa placed it under the tree.

"I have something for you," Anna said.

"Really? I'm excited," Lisa said.

"Do you want to have some dinner first before we open up gifts?" she asked.

"I thought you'd never ask," Lisa said with a smile on her face.

They sat down and had dinner, but Anna noticed Lisa was incredibly quiet. She was looking around, pursing her lips as she spoke.

"Sorry, I'm just excited to give my present to you. I'm very tired, but the look on your face was what drove me forward," she said.

"Really? You didn't have to stay up all night for me," Anna said.

"No, I wanted to. You matter to me right now. You've changed me for the better, and I'm happy that you're in my life," she said.

Anna nodded.

"We've both really come a long way in the last few weeks," Anna said.

"I know we have. And I feel great about it. I've been a little worried, but I know you'll enjoy what I have for you," she said.

The rest of the dinner continued to be quiet, but Anna felt that excitement as it permeated the area, almost like a drug. Lisa had something meaningful for both of them, and she couldn't wait.

After dinner, Lisa went over to the tree that Anna had just put up. She looked at the ornaments that she made with Nina, smiling.

"I'm so glad I made those with her," Lisa said.

"I am too. Nina adores you, Lisa," Anna said.

"And I adore her too. I hope we stick around for a little bit. Together," Lisa said.

"You know I don't want you to leave," Anna said.

"I've been a little on edge about life recently. I've done a lot of thinking and made some incredible changes to my life. It's changed me for the better Anna, and I thank you for it," Lisa said.

"You do?" she said.

"Of course. If it weren't for you, I would have never had a relationship with you. If it weren't for you, I wouldn't have stuck around so long. If it weren't for you, I wouldn't be the happy person I am today. So, I do have you to thank Anna, for pretty much everything," she said.

"I guess the same could be said for you. I mean, I'm happier now than ever before. Peter isn't breathing down my neck to find a relationship. I feel like I'm a better mom to Nina. Everything feels right. Maybe this is the best Christmas gift of them all," she said.

"I think it is. But of course, that's all up to the person at hand. But I did get you something nice, Anna. Something that reminded me of us," she said.

Anna sat down, and Lisa gave her the big present.

"What's this?" Anna asked.

"Something that I made to express my love for you," she said.

Anna opened the gift, immediately shocked at the sight in front of her. It was a painting. It was she and Lisa together, and Nina on the side. The three of them were smiling. It had a wonderful tone. The colors were vibrant. It was so beautiful, it made Anna cry.

Anna felt the happy tears cascade down her face. She wasn't suffering anymore, and as she looked at the image, she felt happy, secure and whole. She noticed a presence behind her, and arms wrapped around her body. Anna lay her head on Lisa's shoulders.

"There we go. We did it," she said.

"We sure did. I love you, Lisa," Anna said.

"I love you, too, Anna," she replied.

There was a small silence. Then, Anna grabbed something from under the tree.

"I got this for you. It's a multi-part gift, and something that makes me happy," she said.

Lisa opened it. Inside was a picture framed. It was the photo they took while in the park. Inside was also a card.

You're the artist I've been searching for, the person who stole my heart, the one who makes me happy and secure. I want to be with you forever. I love you. I hope this support for your career is enough to get it going because I want to see you make beautiful art and stay in my life. Inside was a small piece of paper, and on it, was a key, and a letter. As Lisa read it, she looked at Anna.

"You can't be serious," she said.

"I am Lisa. I talked to Rupert. He told me that if I wanted to support someone using my share of the investment, I can and that someone is you. I want to see you succeed Lisa. I want to see you do well," she said.

Lisa looked too awestruck for words, and Anna beamed. She loved seeing Lisa like that, seeing her completely at the mercy of the words and actions that Anna took, and the choices she made.

"Oh my God, Anna," she said.

"I wanted to give you a great Christmas present. I felt like this was fitting," she said.

Lisa felt her body rise off the ground, arms latched around her, and a bit, meaningful kiss against her lips. When Lisa pulled back, she grinned.

"Thank you, Anna. This is the best Christmas gift anyone could ever give me," Lisa said.

"Merry Christmas! I love you," Anna replied.

Chapter Nineteen

Lisa felt so amazed by the sheer care, generosity and love that Anna had for her. It made her feel whole, made her feel welcome. Lisa also felt ready for whatever life would throw at her next.

Lisa and Anna shared a deep, loving kiss with each other, one that said everything. The pain they went through, the future they had together, it was all right there and Lisa didn't care, she was just ready to finally make Anna happy, no matter what life threw at her.

They had already gone through a lot in a short span of time. Even with all of that in place, Lisa could tell that Anna was trying her very hardest to be the best person that she could be. The way they kissed, the way they shared the tender feeling, it was all that Lisa wanted in life.

Lisa wanted a life partner and she got one with Anna.

When Anna pulled away, a trickle of spit connecting their lips, she flushed.

"Are you good?" Anna asked.

"Perfect. How are you?"

"Amazing. I'm so glad that you're here with me Lisa. You're wonderful," Anna said.

"The feeling is mutual," she said.

"I want to make you feel good tonight. Come with me to the bedroom," she insisted.

Lisa was surprised by the sudden forcefulness of Anna's words, but she wasn't complaining. She took Anna's hand, and together, they made their way up the stairs and to the bedroom. When Anna closed the door, she pinned Lisa down, surprising her with a forceful array of kisses.

"Whoa," she said, shocked at how needy and wanting Anna was. Anna pulled back, blushing slightly.

"Sorry, was it too much?" she asked.

"Not at all, this is just a very pleasant surprise," Lisa said with a smirk.

"Good. Because I've missed this myself," Anna said.

Anna kissed Lisa with a flurry of touches and caresses. Lisa was shocked at how delightful Anna was at kissing. They shared a long, languid kiss. Lisa then let out a small moan, causing Anna to let her tongue slip in, moving against her own lips.

"Oh God," Lisa said, letting her moans mix with Anna's own. The pleasure of the moment was driving them both to madness. Anna then let out a small hum, watching as Lisa then started to let out a series of small groans with every single moment.

"Are you okay?" Anna asked.

"Wonderful," Lisa said, looking at Anna with a smile.

Lisa then kissed her once again. Anna pushed her tongue in, with touching Lisa's body. She moved her hands up to Lisa's nipples which were poking through her shirt. Anna touched them slightly and made Lisa moan.

"Oh my God," Lisa said, slightly surprised by how good Anna was.

"You like that?" Anna inquired.

"That's an understatement," Lisa teased.

"Well I'm just asking," Anna said with a purr.

Anna then teased the edges of her nipples with her hands, followed by her lips. Lisa felt like she was about to lose all control of her body. Anna's kisses down her body were delightful, almost like a treat that only she could take part in. The moment was solidified in Lisa's mind, making her shudder with delight as she felt a small grasp on her neck, the sucking sensation following it.

"Oh God," Lisa said to herself, feeling like everything was driving her to the point of madness. It was making her shiver and making her lose everything within her. It took all her willpower just to make herself hold back, and she could tell that Anna was smiling in pleasure as she continued her actions.

"Anna, why are you so damn perfect?" Lisa asked.

"Because you love me," she said.

The laugh that came out of Lisa's lips immediately made Anna pull back.

"What's funny? Did I say something wrong?"

"Not at all, Anna. You're just so perfect it's not even funny," she said.

"Really?" she asked.

"Really. You make me happy. For the first time in a long time, I feel really secure. It's wonderful to finally fall in love again and make love to a wonderful woman," Lisa said.

"Well, I'll take care of you tonight, since you were so nice the first time," Anna said.

Anna moved her lips downward, giving those delightful kisses once again. It took all of Lisa's willpower not to let her body lose control right then and there. But, she didn't want to just yet. Lisa was excited to feel the effects of it, to feel the sudden, rapturous pleasure that came.

Lisa was losing all semblance of control as Anna continued to tease her. Anna moved her hand to Lisa's shirt, deftly pulling it off. Anna's hands again touched her nipples, teasing them slightly. She watched as Lisa let out a sudden moan.

"Aww, they're so sensitive. I love it," Anna said, touching and teasing Lisa's nipples with both her lips and her hands.

The stimulation was enough to drive Lisa crazy. She could feel her control starting to slip away as she felt Anna continue the onslaught against her body. Lisa then started to shiver, enjoying the feeling. With every moment, she could feel everything start to change within her, making her cry out in pleasure at the feeling. Anna's hands were perfect, her lips sublime. Lisa wanted to just sit here at the moment, feeling the effects of everything Anna did to her.

Anna wasn't done yet. She then moved her hands downward, moving toward Lisa's heat and cupping it. It was a different pace compared to Lisa, who was a bit rougher around the edges. Anna had a touch that was so light, so serine and amazing that Lisa couldn't help but shiver as she became putty in Anna's hands.

Anna then moved her hands to Lisa's pants, undoing the buttons, then slipping them off her body. Lisa started to cry out, suddenly feeling the aching urge for everything to just continue right then and there. Anna then again moved her hands to Lisa's honey pot, lightly playing with the outer area from the outside of her panties. The small touches and stimulations against Lisa's sex were enough to drive Lisa to the brink. She felt her entire body lose control, felt everything grow a lot stronger within her, and Lisa couldn't help but love it.

Anna was so skilled with her hands. Each touch, each stimulation, each rub and push made Lisa shiver with delight. She cried out in wanton pleasure. Lisa found herself wanting Anna to just completely overtake her body and make her want to experience the full gamut of love and desire. Just as Lisa was about to completely lose it, Anna stopped.

Anna pulled away, pulling Lisa's panties down. Then Anna opened Lisa's legs and put her lips against her heat. She watched with delight as Lisa started to cry out, each stroke making her pull her hands to Anna's head. Lisa was completely amazed and aroused by it all, suddenly enjoying everything at hand.

Lisa was already close. Anna again stopped. She pulled back and started to undress herself.

"What are you doing?" Lisa asked, slightly breathless from the actions at hand.

"Taking care of both of us tonight. I found a new toy and I wanted to try it with you," she said with a smile on her face

Lisa wondered just what it was. Then Anna pulled it out. It was a double-ended dildo. Lisa blushed. She had never tried using something like that. Fingers and mouth were her choices of doing things.

As Anna started to move her hands toward her entrance while holding the toy, Lisa smiled.

"I can help," Lisa teased.

"All right," Anna said, letting Lisa take the toy and push it in. The stretch was a welcome feeling. Lisa moaned. Anna then moved to the other side, getting on it and pushing down.

Together, they both started to move against each other, their hands, mouths and bodies intertwining together. They touched each other's breasts and their sensitive spots. Each touch made them both cry out in pleasure and need. For Lisa, her body was completely enraptured by the feelings.

They continued to kiss and tease each other. Anna pulled back, looking at Lisa with a smile on her face.

"I love you. This is the best moment ever," Anna said.

"I love you too, I'll be there for you, and I'll make sure you're taken care of, no matter what," Lisa said.

They continued to move in synchronization with each other, both of them moaning in complete desire and pleasure, both of them adjusting to each of the feelings for the other person without stopping. The pleasure in their bodies, the movement at hand, and the experiences that they were having, were all too much. After a few more moments, Anna then moved forward, crushing their lips together as they both came together.

For Lisa, it was the end of an old life and the beginning of a new life. For Anna, she could tell that she was finally moving on. Anna was definitely happier, at least from the look on her face. When she finally came down from her orgasm, Lisa then looked at her with a smile. For a moment, neither of them said anything. Then, Lisa spoke.

"Are you doing okay?" Lisa asked.

"Yeah. Amazing actually," Anna said.

"Good. I'm definitely happy with the way things are going for both of us," She said.

"Same here. I'm happy to have finally moved on. After so long, I can finally press forward," she said.

"That's the spirit. That's what we're going for here. Not to be held back by our pasts, and to finally move on with our lives. I'm here now. I'm not held back by the ghosts of my pasts. I'm happy to have you in my life," she said.

"I am too, Lisa. I'm glad I can finally be myself. I can finally have a complete loving family, and a woman who matters to me."

"The feeling is mutual," Lisa said.

They kissed. For a bit, they sat down and just talked about the sweet nothings of life. For Lisa, she knew that this was the beginning of a new, immersive life for her. She had Anna in her life, so everything would be okay.

That was what she told herself. That no matter what came forth, and whatever happened next, it would all be okay. Anna was here, and together, they would build the best life they could for themselves, and the best experiences possible.

Chapter Twenty

The next day, Anna woke up, holding Lisa's hand as they stared at each other. "Merry Christmas," Lisa said.

"Merry Christmas to you, too," Anna replied, smiling at her new girlfriend.

They kissed, cuddling up next to each other. Anna realized just how perfect it was. It felt so nice, a welcoming feeling, and it was a different kind of love from what she experienced in the past.

***

Lisa and Anna got up shortly afterward and got ready to go over to Peter's house for Christmas dinner. Peter said that dinner would be at three. He also said that they would have their own little celebration beforehand.

They drove to Peter's house. When they got there, they got out the car and walked up to the front door. Anna knocked on the door. Peter quickly answered the door.

"There you are! Merry Christmas," he said.

"Merry Christmas to you. Peter, I know your first meeting wasn't under the best situation. This is Lisa by the way," Anna said.

Lisa nodded, and Peter smiled.

"Well hello, Lisa. Merry Christmas to you!" Peter said.

"Thank you. You, too, Peter," she said.

They went inside, and when they arrived, an older woman was in the kitchen.

"You obviously know my mother, Anna. Lisa, this is my mother, Terri. She's helping me out until I can get back on my feet and all," he said.

"Hello, there ladies. How have you been Anna?" she said.

"A lot better. Thanks, Terri," Anna said.

She was happy that they were at least on decent terms with the ex-in-laws and such. When Nina came over, she raced to Anna, and Anna hugged her.

"Merry Christmas sweetie!" she said.

"Thanks, Mommy," she said.

"Did Santa get you everything"

"Of course! I'm very happy. And I opened your gifts, Mommy. They're wonderful," she said.

"Wonderful. I'm glad," Anna said.

"Oh, and this is for you. Lisa helped me figure out what to get you," she said.

Anna looked at the box, surprised that she even got her anything. Nina was a young child, so it usually was something she crafted. This time there was a box.

"Open it! Open it!"

"All right I will," Anna said with a laugh.

She opened the box, and in there was a beautiful turquoise stone.

"How did you—"

"I helped with it. She told me that you would love it. The stone is so beautiful. I also included it in our picture, but I don't think you realized it," Lisa said.

Anna touched the stone, her eyes widening.

"Thank you. Both of you. You both make me feel loved," she said.

"We try our best," Lisa said.

She gave them both a hug, giving them kisses. When Anna gave Peter his gift, a necktie, he smiled.

"You always know what to get me, Anna," he said.

"You're simple, that's why I do it," she said with a smile.

It was so weird to be on such good terms with everyone, but she wasn't going to complain. This was the best Christmas together in a long time.

As they sat down and spoke, the conversation was nice and friendly. It was so odd how two very different families could come together and work it out. Anna was just happy she had someone in her life, someone everyone liked and someone she saw a bright future with.

Christmas wishes really can come true!

Manufactured by Amazon.ca
Bolton, ON